just for you

just for you

escape to new zealand, prequel novella

ROSALIND JAMES

author's note

The Blues and the All Blacks are actual rugby teams. However, this is a work of fiction. Names, characters, places, and incidents are products of the author's imagination or are used fictitiously and are not to be construed as real. Any resemblance to actual events or persons, living or dead, is entirely coincidental.

table of contents

new zealand map

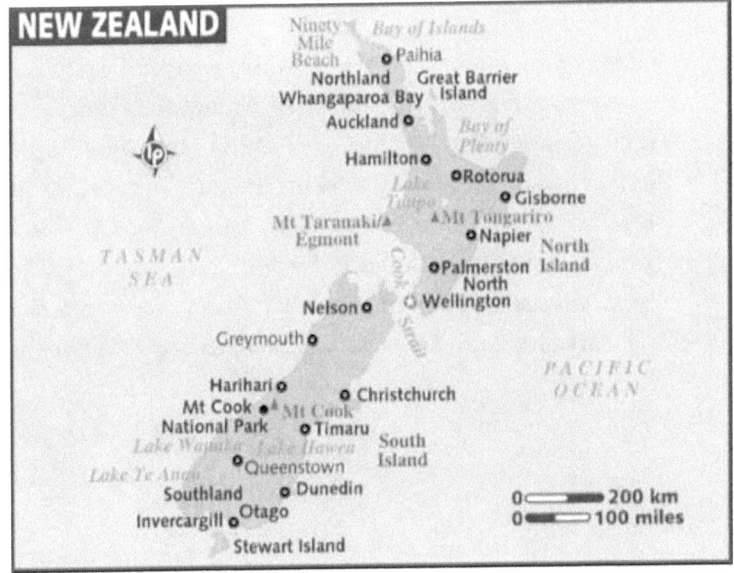

Note: A New Zealand glossary appears at the end of this book.

No shirt, no shoes, no...problems?

Hemi Ranapia isn't looking for love. Fun, yes. Love, not so much. But a summer fishing holiday to laid-back Russell could turn out to be more adventure than this good-time boy ever bargained for.

Reka Harata hasn't forgotten the disastrously hot rugby star she met a year ago, no matter how much she wishes she could. Too bad Hemi keeps refusing to be left in her past.

Sometimes, especially in New Zealand's Maori Northland, it really does take a village. And sometimes it just takes a little faith.

From the Author: This 36,000-word (120-page) novella begins about six years before the events of *Just This Once*. It was designed to be read as a stand-alone book and an intro to the series—but if you've read the others and are curious, here's a handy-dandy little guide to familiar characters you'll wave "hi" to in this story:

Drew Callahan (Blues): 24, like Hemi; just made captain of the Blues.
Finn Douglas (Blues): 27.
Nate Torrance (Hurricanes): 21.
Liam (Mako) Mahaka (Hurricanes): 20.
Kevin McNicholl (Blues): 19.

> (And yes, they do start playing that
> young! It's a young man's sport.)

blast from the past

♡

The baby was crying, but that wasn't why he was watching.

Hemi Ranapia leant against the rail on the upper deck of the car ferry that had left Opua a few minutes earlier and would be in Okiato in a few more. He wasn't looking at the placid waters of the Bay of Islands with his mates, though, or paying attention to their desultory conversation about the fishing trip they had planned for the next day. He was watching the girl.

Because he'd met her before. He'd done more than meet her, and he remembered it pretty well. That part would have been a good memory. That part *was* a good memory. The part that was worrying him was the baby.

She hadn't noticed him yet. She was walking on the opposite side of the ferry's top deck, holding the crying baby, talking or singing to it, he couldn't tell. She was moving in his direction, every step a swaying bounce to calm the fussing infant, and one part of him wanted to go below, but the other part kept him rooted, waiting for her to recognize him.

He saw the moment she did, the moment her large, liquid brown eyes met his own, the moment her feet stopped moving.

She bounced the baby a bit more, but absently now. Aaron and Nikau stopped chatting about fishing and looked at her, and, baby or not, Hemi knew why they were looking, because she looked like a flower, something tropical and lush. She was wearing a flouncy pale-green skirt and a pretty orange top that clung to her rich figure, and her hair, pulled back into its Maori knot, was every bit as dark and shining, her skin every bit as velvety brown, her curves every bit as luscious as they'd looked in the red bridesmaid's dress she'd been wearing the last time he'd seen her. The dress she'd been wearing for a while, anyway.

"Hemi," she said, and it wasn't an invitation.

He froze, because he couldn't remember her name. He could remember every single detail of what she'd looked like naked, what she'd looked like under him, but for the life of him, he couldn't remember her name.

"You have a baby," he said, and if there was a stupider opening line, he didn't know what it would be. Now that she was closer, he could see that it was a Maori baby, but that was about it. Which left the question exactly as open as it had been before.

Another woman was approaching her, holding a curly-haired boy of about five by one hand and piloting an empty pushchair with the other. She reached for the still-crying baby, and the girl handed him—her? over.

"Thanks, love," the other woman said. "Let's go downstairs and get in the car, Tai," she told the little boy. "Tamati needs a feed."

A boy, then. Hemi watched the little family leave, looked back at the girl again. "Not your baby."

"No," she said, and the relief filled him. At least there was that.

"Hi." Aaron jumped straight into the gap. "You know Hemi, do you? This holiday's getting better all the time. I'm Aaron."

She looked at him, hesitated a moment, and Hemi wasn't sure she was even going to answer.

"Reka," she said at last, and he closed his eyes for a second and cursed his faulty memory. Of course. Reka. "Sweet." She'd been that and then some.

She wasn't looking sweet now, though. She cast him a dismissive glance and followed her friend through the doorway that led down the stairs to the car deck beneath, and that was that. The end of their second meeting.

mistakes happen

♡

The pub on the ground floor of the Duke of Marlborough Hotel was hopping. Summer was always a busy time in the tourist town of Russell, despite its isolated location at the tip of a peninsula, barely accessible except by ferry, bang in the middle of the Bay of Islands and a good three and a half hours' drive north of Auckland.

If summer was busy, a Saturday night in mid-January was the busiest, and Reka Harata was rushed off her feet. She wiped down a table that a hovering group hurried to occupy, then turned to the next, held down solidly by a group of American tourists.

"Care for another?" she asked them.

"Well, let's see," a sixtyish man with a belly said. "We've got noplace to go but back to the hotel, and plenty of sports on TV. I think I'm getting the hang of this rugby thing. I could watch this all night. What do you all think?" he asked his companions. "Another beer sound good to everyone?"

"Oh, I don't know," his wife dithered. "Do you think it's a good idea?"

Reka waited, patient smile intact, as the three couples made their decisions. She was finally able to collect their dirty

4

glasses and head back to the bar for the refills they'd decided on—the refills she'd known they'd decide on. She didn't know why Americans always had to pretend they didn't really want to drink. Kiwis and Aussies had no such qualms.

Her step faltered a bit at the sight of the two men entering the crowded, noisy room. They found a spot at one side of a big table facing the widescreen TV that was showing the Sevens tournament in Wellington, the sound off because it couldn't have been heard anyway. Hemi and one of his mates, in her section. Of course he was.

She went back to the bar, deposited the dirty glasses and collected drinks for another table from Fred, and headed out again. Head high, a little extra sway to her walk. Not needing him to notice her. Not needing any man here. Too good for all of them. The posture was familiar, even if it came harder tonight.

But the whole time she was serving drinks, taking orders, her mind was back there anyway, no matter how much she tried to stop it.

She'd noticed him even while she'd been walking down the aisle in the wharenui, wearing the stupid strapless dress of blood-red satin that Victoria had chosen, a dress she was definitely not going to be wearing again, a dress that had "bridesmaid" written all over it. She'd been supposed to be paying attention to her pace, and instead she'd been looking at the man sitting at the end of the row, up there to her right. A man who was looking right back at her. A mate of the groom's, she knew, because Victoria had told them all he was coming.

Hemi Ranapia, the starting No. 10 for the Auckland Blues, one of the year's new caps for the All Blacks, and about the finest specimen of Maori manhood she'd ever seen. His dark, wavy hair cut short and neat, his brown eyes alive with interest as he watched her. A physique to die for, too, his shoulders broad in the black suit, his waistline trim, the size of his arms and thighs making it clear that the suit hadn't come off any rack, because that had taken some extra material.

She'd stood in her neat row to one side of the bride throughout the service, had done her best to keep her attention on the event, and had felt his gaze on her as surely as if he'd been touching her. She'd had to will herself not to shiver, and the look he sent her way, unsmiling and intent, when she walked back up the aisle again told her she hadn't been imagining his interest.

She'd still had what felt like hours of photo-taking to come. Standing around endlessly, smiling in the sunshine, arranging and rearranging herself according to the photographer's instructions, being flirted with by one of the groomsmen, with Hemi in and out of her view all the while. His suit coat off now, his tie loosened, white shirt stretching across chest and shoulders. A beer in his hand and a smile on his face, having a chat with the other boys, being approached, at first shyly and then with enthusiasm, by the kids. And by the girls, she saw with a twinge of jealousy that made no sense at all, as one after another of them smiled for him, touched her hair, touched his arm. It looked to her like every unattached woman at the wedding, and more than one of the partnered ones as well, was going out of her way to chat him up. And he wasn't exactly resisting.

But he was looking at her all the same. Every now and then, she glanced across and his gaze caught hers, and she saw an expression on his face, an intensity and a heat that were making her burn.

By the time the photography was done and she was released at last, the wedding party moving into the wharekai so the eating and drinking and dancing could begin, she was well and truly warmed up, and tingling more than a little in every single place she could imagine him touching with those clever hands, the hands she somehow knew would handle a woman as deftly as they handled a rugby ball.

The band began to play, the bride and groom stepped into their first dance, and she saw him edging his way around an animated group towards her, a glass in each hand. He reached her side, handed her the flute of champagne with the flash of a smile.

"Think you earned this," he told her.

She took it, and he touched his glass to hers.

"Cheers," he said with another white smile, the heat in his gaze unmistakable at this range. He tipped his brown throat back and drank, and she mirrored his action, felt golden bubbles popping against her tongue, the cool liquid sliding down her own throat. Drinking together like that somehow felt as intimate as kissing him, and the tongues of flame were licking every secret spot now.

"Took your time, didn't you?" she asked him with a cool she wasn't even close to feeling.

He laughed. "Didn't want to seem too eager. Doing my best to be smooth here, but it's hard going."

Another long drink, another long look as Victoria and Mason finished their dance and the band began another number, a fast one, and couples started filling the floor.

"Think I can get a dance?" he asked.

"Mmm, I think you could," she said. "Maybe so."

He smiled again, took her glass from her and set it on the table, then led her out onto the floor, his big hand closing around her own, and she looked up at the strong column of his throat, the vee of brown skin at its base where he had opened a button, and wanted to put her mouth there.

They danced fast, and they danced slow, and he started out holding her with a firm hand at her waist, the other still wrapped around hers. It started out all right, like any other dance with any other man.

She hadn't fallen as fast as she could have. She'd made him work for it at least that much, had danced with other fellas, had turned away from him and not looked at him for whole numbers at a time. But all the same, a few more glasses of champagne and more than a few dances later, she was in his arms without a molecule of air separating them, and her hands were sliding over those shoulders, that back, feeling the strength and the heat of him through the thin white cotton, and his hands were on her hips, and the two of them were barely swaying.

He pulled back a bit, and she looked up at him, and something happened.

He wasn't smiling anymore. He was looking at her, just looking. Their eyes met, locked, and the connection was a physical thing, as if a cord were wrapped around them, binding them together. She felt it in her chest, her belly, and everywhere else, too, and the big, crowded room full of music and laughter and people faded away until it was just the two of them, just this one moment, just Hemi looking at her.

"Get a bit of air," he said when the song ended, and she walked straight out the door with him. Around the back of the wharekai, her hand still in his, until they rounded the corner and were in the darkest shadows, in a depression where the pipes came out of the wall, and he was pulling her into his arms.

His lips were warm and firm, and when they touched hers, she felt the contact all the way through her sensitized body. His mouth took hers in a hot, slow, sweet kiss, then traveled across her cheek to her neck, to the perfect spot beneath her ear, and she moaned, because it felt so good. She was liquid inside, and more than inside.

They kissed like that for long minutes in the warm air of the summer night, a light breeze caressing them, the darkness embracing them, the sky an overturned bowl pricked in ten thousand places to let ten thousand tiny lights shine through. And when one big hand strayed down from her waist to cup her bottom, to stroke over the curve of her, all she felt was pleasure at the touch, all she wanted was to move even closer. So she did, though she didn't really have to, because he was hauling her up against him with all the strength of that big arm. And when the other hand didn't even bother with the boning at her bodice, just dove straight inside to close around a breast, his palm moving over a nipple that had been hard and aching for his touch since the first time he'd looked at her in the wharenui, she was so far past protesting, all she could do was turn her head to the side so he could bite her neck some more.

She felt herself being walked backwards, and she was against the wooden wall. She could feel the vibration, hear the throbbing music coming from inside, matched by the throb at her core. He was pulling up her skirt by the hand-ful, and then his hand was underneath it, his touch like a brand, rubbing over her, burning her, and she wanted more.

"Wet," he said on a sigh. "Aw, that's good. You're so wet for me." He kept touching her there, kept kissing her, and she was gasping into his mouth, because his hand had slid beneath the lace band at the leg opening, and he was there. And, oh, did he know how to pet her, how to stroke her in exactly the way she needed.

And then he settled down to the business of making her come, because he was talking.

"This is so sweet," he told her. "So hot. So wet. It's all for me, isn't it? You're going to give it all to me, aren't you? You're going to give it all up to me tonight."

She couldn't answer, because she was past it. Her breath was coming in sobbing gasps, and then she was being carried away by great waves of pleasure, riding his hand as he held her up, took her all the way.

She was leaning against the wall, catching her breath, and his hands were at his belt, then unzipping, and somehow her underwear wasn't there anymore, and he was lifting her.

"Wrap your legs around me," he told her, and she gave another gasp and obeyed, and he slid home. Her back was against the wall, and he was inside her, hard and fast and a little bit rough, and the music played inside and the warmth of the Northland night was no match for the heat that was Hemi filling her, taking her up again with the forbidden excitement of it, and she was trying not to cry out, taken over again by the raw pleasure that was pushing her higher, and higher still.

As she surrendered to it, she could feel him being pulled down with her into the dark, his gasping breaths coming in time with her own, his hands tightening beneath her until she could tell they would leave marks, and he was coming too, hard and fast and, with a groan, pulling her into the grip of one final, highest wave that receded only slowly, left her shuddering in its wake.

He set her on her feet again, got rid of the condom, and she reached shaking hands to adjust her dress, to try to tidy her hair. Remembered that her undies were on the ground, and couldn't find them in the dark.

He crouched down himself, put a hand out for them, handed them to her. "Let's get out of here," he told her. "I have a room."

He did. And for the rest of the night, he showed her that he knew how to do it more ways than fast and hard. That he knew exactly how to make a woman feel good, and that he was willing to take his slow, sweet time to do it, until she was wrung out, shattered, limp with pleasure.

Until the morning, when he told her that he had to get back to Auckland for training. When he drove her back to her hotel, kissed her goodbye, told her he'd call. When he'd driven away, and straight out of her life.

And the whole thing nobody's fault but her own.

♡

Well, mistakes happened, and she wasn't crying into her pillow one minute more over this one. So she walked over to his table, one long year later, gave the rings of condensation from the previous occupants' glasses a brisk wipe with the wet bar cloth, and asked the two men, her gaze somewhere between them, "What can I get you?'

She didn't get an answer, because a voice came from behind her. "Ah. The beautiful Reka. Must be my lucky night."

She felt him before she turned, because he was standing much too close, right up in her space. The other man from the ferry, Aaron, she remembered. Another rugby player, and he thought he was playing now. He was already drunk, and he was smiling, too.

She stepped back a pace and ignored him. "What can I get you boys?" she repeated.

"How about a bit of you?" Aaron asked. He reached a hand out and grabbed her bum, gave it a squeeze, pulled her towards him.

She didn't think, just hauled off and slapped the bar cloth backhanded across his face with as much force as she could manage, straight across his nose and mouth.

He staggered back at the clammy touch of the wet rag, came up spluttering.

"Keep your bloody hands off me," she told him, her voice shaking with rage. "Next time you grab me like that, I'll have a knife in that hand. Dead hard to catch a rugby ball when you're missing a couple fingers."

He was lunging for her, reaching out to grab her arm, and Fred was at her side.

"Problem?" the bartender growled, his voice like iron.

Hemi and the other fella had jumped up as well, though, and Hemi had Aaron's arm in a grip so hard it must have been painful, had yanked him back from Reka.

"No problem," Hemi said. "We're just leaving."

"Too right you are," Fred said. "I don't care who the hell you are, that's not on. You're out."

Reka shot Hemi one more look and took herself on over to the next table. He'd probably told Aaron that she was an easy mark. Heaven knew she had been. He might have had more finesse than his mate, but the idea was the same. Just another sportsman looking to get it quick and easy. Well, he wasn't going to get it from her. Not this time.

the thrill of the chase

♡

"Reka working tonight?"

The bartender continued pulling the beer from the tap without looking up. Hemi was pretty sure the man had heard, so he waited as patiently as he could manage.

It was the same fella who'd thrown them out the night before. Balding, grizzled, and tough as teak. He finished pouring the beer, put the schooner on the tray with the rest of the drinks, waited until a waitress had hustled up to grab it before he spoke. "Nah. Not here."

"Any idea where I could find her, then?" Hemi persisted. "Or when she *will* be working? Tomorrow?"

"Look, mate." The man stopped cleaning the bar with a cloth and looked up. "You want a beer, you're welcome. But I don't go around offering up a girl's whereabouts to every randy fella who wants to know, no matter what kind of boot he's got."

"I knew her before, though," Hemi tried to explain.

"Not my business," the bartender said. "Didn't get the impression she was too keen on you last night, and I wasn't either, not on you or your mates. Now, you want a beer or not?"

"Not," Hemi sighed, and turned to go.

It wasn't turning into the holiday of his dreams. The fishing charter had been hampered a bit by Aaron spewing over the side for half the journey, a hangover giving some extra punch to a pretty spectacular bout of seasickness. They'd gone out blue-water fishing for hapuku anyway without a bit of success, had contented themselves at the end of the day with a few snapper, which they'd barbecued and shared with a family of tourists picnicking at the Reserve, because that had been a fair bit of fish.

Which was all good, all very relaxing for his holiday, all part of the plan. And right now, Nikau and a somewhat sober Aaron were at the Wharf, having a beer and no doubt meeting girls, which was the other point of the holiday.

Aaron had been pretty cavalier about the whole Reka episode once he'd got over the initial flash of anger, which had enraged Hemi at the time. But then, that was Aaron, and Reka had been just been another girl to him. Just another girl.

When Hemi had seen him grabbing her bum, though…he'd wanted to hit him himself, only Reka had beat him to it. He hadn't been able to stomach any more of him that night, but it had passed, because Aaron was a teammate, and a mate as well, and he'd been pissed, and he hadn't known.

Hadn't known what, Hemi wasn't sure. Not that any of it mattered, because there the two other boys were, having a good time, and here he was, trying to find a girl who, the bartender was right, hadn't seemed any too keen on renewing his acquaintance.

"Oi. Mate."

Hemi turned. The speaker was an older man, perched on a stool at one end of the long wooden bar as if it were his habitual spot, which it probably was.

"She's helping out her auntie tomorrow at the Vortex Training Café," the man told him. "Heard her say so, last night."

"Where's that?" Hemi asked.

The man snorted. "Where? Up the road a bit. It's bloody Russell, mate."

"Cheers," Hemi said, and took himself off. To the Wharf, where he did have a couple beers, and did meet girls, because Nikau and Aaron had found themselves a lively group of backpackers and were chatting up a couple of fit Germans and a pretty spectacular Swede. And Hemi, who had spoken a grand total of two sentences to Reka that she'd barely deigned to answer, was the only one who went back to his room alone, which didn't make any sense at all.

"Haere mai," the middle-aged woman behind the counter said, the next midday.

"Kia ora." Hemi stepped aside to let a curly-haired toddler dressed only in a nappy march out with a deter-mined waddle from behind the counter to a table where two young women were sitting.

A couple teenagers wandered through next with a nod to the woman, so casual that Hemi couldn't tell whether they were family or staff, and he had to smile a little. It was good to be in familiar territory. He looked at the menu printed on a blackboard behind the counter. "What's good?"

"Hamburger and chips," the woman said with a smile of her own. "Best to stick with the basics. It's a training café, eh."

"I'll have that, then," Hemi decided. "And a beer."

As he pulled out his card to pay, he asked, as casually as he could manage, "Would you be Reka's auntie, by any chance? Is she about somewhere?"

The older woman's gaze sharpened a bit. "I would be. And who would you be?"

"Hemi Ranapia."

"Thought you looked familiar. Here on holiday?"

"Yeh." He saw her waiting expectantly, and went on. He wouldn't even get his beer, much less a chance at a chat with Reka, he got the feeling, until she got her answer. "I saw Reka the other day, when I was arriving on the ferry. I'd met her before, as it happens."

"On the ferry? Oh, when she was coming back with my daughter. They had to take that scamp Tai to Kawakawa to get his cast off." The woman's posture suggested that she could chat for any length of time. "That boy's capable of breaking an arm again just walking down the surgery steps. Decide to come down it on his skateboard on his belly, like as not. That's how he did the arm, on the skateboard. You never know what's next. And with the baby and all, Ana needed the help."

"Yeh, saw that," Hemi said, trying to stay patient. "Her holding the baby, I mean. I was hoping I'd see her again today."

The woman's glance was shrewd. "I'll see if I can find her," she said, although Hemi suspected that, if Reka were on the premises, that wouldn't be too difficult. It was a pretty tiny place.

There were a couple groups queueing behind him, though, so he headed out to the umbrella-shaded patio with a final "Cheers" and hoped for the best, stepping around the toddler again along the way, since the little fella had decided to sit himself down in the middle of the doorway.

♡

He amused himself by watching the parade of tourists along the footpath lining the grandly named but ridiculously narrow York Street. The more conscientious, consulting guidebooks or signs, seemed to be heading for the museum and the Anglican church that, he knew, was New Zealand's oldest. Pretty ironic, considering that this was the town once known as the "Hellhole of the Pacific."

Times had changed since those early roistering whaling days, though, because now, it was anything but. An idyllically pretty—and incredibly sleepy—seaside village with not much to offer beyond beach, fishing, and gift shops.

He looked up as a plate holding a moderately acceptable hamburger and pile of chips was slid in front of him, and saw Reka setting down his beer and a glass to go with it.

"Cheers," he said. "I was hoping to find you here."

"That's what Auntie Kiri said, though I can't think why," she answered. "Didn't exactly try to find me before this, did you?"

"Could you..." He paused a moment. She was here, so what did he do now? "Could you sit with me, have a beer?"

"I'm working."

"A fizz, then. A cuppa. A coffee. Whatever."

"No, I mean I'm working, and it's lunchtime, and it's summer. I can't have a chat even if I wanted to."

"Right, then. Dinner?"

"Don't think so." She picked up the tray she'd set on the table and turned to go.

"Reka, wait." He put out a protesting hand, but he didn't touch her, because he was getting the picture. "I'm trying to ask you out. Properly."

"Good of you, but I'm not interested."

She walked away, and he turned in his seat to watch her go. Another skirt, jandals, a sleeveless turquoise blouse, all of it showing off her firm, shapely arms and legs, her spectacular curves. Her hair knotted at the back of her head. Hair that, he knew, reached to her waist in thick waves of the darkest brown when she took it down. Or when he did.

He'd stood behind her in the hotel room on that warm summer evening, had slid the zip of that red dress slowly down her back, had watched it fall to the floor in a crimson pool, leaving her standing in nothing but high heels and a pair of undies that he'd already taken off once and couldn't wait to take off again, and he'd held her by the shoulders, bent to kiss her neck from behind. Had pressed up close behind her, a hand going around to cup a full, round breast as if he couldn't help himself, because he couldn't. Had felt her shiver under his mouth, his touch, feeling her as attuned to him as he was to her, like they were connected, like he was in her skin and she was in his.

He'd pulled the pins out of her hair, then, one by one, watched the dark, curling mass fall down her brown back until it reached the devastatingly deep curve of her waist, and he'd plunged his hands into it, pulled her head gently back by it and kissed her neck again, and that had been the start of their second time.

Not their last time that night, but the last time he was likely to see, at the rate he was going. He sighed, picked up his hamburger, and asked himself why it mattered. He'd thought in the past that the first time was the best, or the second at most. The excitement of the hunt, the chase. But he'd already done that, with her. He'd caught her, he'd had her, and he'd let her go.

The problem was, he wanted to catch her again, and this time, he wanted to hold her. But she wasn't playing anymore.

a bit of holiday fun

♡

He woke early the next morning because, once again, he'd gone to bed early, sober, and alone. He rolled out of bed in his boxers, opened the curtains to another crystalline Northland day, heard the tui offering up their melodious calls in the red-blossomed pohutukawa trees, and decided that he wasn't going to spend another minute of this last day of his holiday in this pokey room. So he pulled on togs and a T-shirt, shoved his feet into jandals and grabbed a towel, thought about taking the car, and decided to walk.

Well, jog, because somehow he always ended up jogging, even in jandals. Walking was so *slow.* Ten minutes over the hill, seeing a few early-morning drivers, a dog-walker or two along the way, and he had turned down the steep track through the bush to Long Beach. A few more quick steps, a hop down the bank, and he was kicking off the jandals and dropping the towel onto the beach, only a couple holidaymakers visible in the distance, a single swimmer in the water making pretty good progress toward shore.

The swimmer's strong crawl brought her closer, and he stopped walking. She stood up in the water that reached just above her knees, and it was Reka.

Reka, in a bright yellow bikini that was doing some hard work to keep her naughty bits covered, and Reka had some *very* naughty bits. Her hair in a long braid, the water glistening on her brown skin, the wet fabric clinging, and he stood for a moment and just looked.

Finally, though, he walked towards her, and she saw him and stopped where she was, at the edge of the water.

"Morning," he said. "I was just about to have a swim myself." Another bloody brilliant opening line.

She glanced at him, then turned away, headed up the shore toward her things. "I see that."

"I could miss that out, though," he said, keeping pace with her, "if you'd like to go for brekkie with me, as we're both here. You're an early riser too, eh."

"Thanks," she said, "but no. I meant what I said yesterday. Not interested."

She bent to her towel on the beach, and despite his frustration, he couldn't help noticing that Reka bending down was a sight for sore eyes. A sight he'd seen before, without the bikini, and a rush of heat filled him at the memory. Reka from behind, bent over the bed, holding on...that had very nearly been his favorite.

But just now, she wasn't bending over anymore. She wasn't trying to show him anything at all. She was drying off with her towel, which he'd have liked to have been helping her with, and then, to his disappointment, she was taking a dress from her bag and pulling it over her head, and all those lush curves were covered again.

"Do you have a partner now, is that it?" he asked. Why hadn't that occurred to him? Because he hadn't wanted to think about it, that was why. And because it didn't even matter now that he had thought of it, which was wrong of him, maybe, but true all the same.

"It couldn't be," she said, facing him again, "that I just don't want *you?* Am I the only girl who's said no, then? Bit hard to believe."

He felt the flush rising. "Of course not. But you wanted me once, and it was good. It was bloody good, and you know it."

"One time," she said.

"More than one time," he pointed out.

"One night," she amended. "And, what? You want one more night? Here you are on holiday again, and here I am, still looking good and so convenient?"

Which was the truth, but somehow not all of the truth. He was struggling to answer that, but she wasn't done.

"I don't think so," she told him. "I'm not interested in being your bit of holiday fun. Again. Shouldn't have done it the first time, but I reckon a girl's allowed one mistake, and you were mine."

He did his best to rally. "That's what it was? A mistake? Seemed to me it was more than that. Felt pretty good, for a mistake."

She looked at him, the scorn coming off her in waves. "Haven't you learnt any more than that, then? Mistakes can feel good. At the time. It's what comes afterwards that lets you know if it's a mistake or not. And what came afterwards between us?"

"Nothing," he admitted. "Nothing."

"Too right."

"Because I didn't call."

"You're quick, aren't you? Yeh, because you didn't call. I can't exactly whinge about that, though, can I? I let somebody shag me against the wall a couple hours after I meet him, and I think he's going to be sending me flowers the next day? Like I said. My mistake, which I'm not interested in making again."

"But I'm...I'm different," he tried to explain. "That was before. That was that first year."

"That first year of what?"

"When I was first selected for the All Blacks. When I was first getting a bit of notice, and everybody wanted to be with me."

Now she was the one flushing. "Like me."

"Nah. Not like you. With you, it was...it was me. I got that. And it was you." He wasn't explaining himself well at all. "I mean, it was special. It wasn't because of the footy thing. It was because it was so good to dance with you, and there was something there, with us. I know there was."

"Huh." It was very nearly a snort. "Pretty bloody special. Here's what actually happened. You're on holiday for a few days. You're leaving, what, today? Tomorrow? You saw me, and you remembered that you had fun, because I'll do anything, and you want to have another 'special' time before you go. And that's all."

"Nah," he found himself saying. "I'm staying on for another couple days." He was? He was going to be taking the bus back, then, because the car was Nikau's, and the boys were leaving today. "I'd make it more," he hurried to add, "but I have to get back to Auckland for training. This is my last bit of time before the season. So have a heart. Go out with me, that's all I'm asking. No strings."

"You want to go out with me? All right, then." She picked up her bag, turned to leave. "I'll be having a bit of a beach day here, tomorrow around noon with my family. You want to see me? See me then."

family matters

♡

She didn't expect him to turn up, of course. She helped Great-Uncle Matiu over the bit of dune and set up a chair for him, spread out a couple blankets for the rest of them, took herself into the water for a swim and barely looked around, because she didn't want to be disappointed.

But when she got out fifteen minutes later, there he was again, watching her. He waited for her to dry off, stood back until she introduced him to her family. She watched him greet Great-Uncle Matiu with a respectful hongi and handshake before turning to Auntie Kiri, then Ana and Ella, another cousin who'd come along for the day. Nothing wrong with his manners, nothing at all.

Nothing wrong with how he looked, either. In togs again, thankfully not too long, which let her look at his thighs, at every hard, delineated muscle of them. She'd seen him on TV in his rugby shorts, and those were even shorter, but the effect was nothing to seeing him up close. His body was, if anything, stronger than the one she remembered. Extra time in the gym, she guessed. And just to make it better, he was wearing an NBA tank top that showed off the solid beef of his shoulders and arms.

The whole effect was pretty overwhelming, and had Ana looking at Reka with a raised eyebrow that Reka ignored.

He'd turned up. She hadn't thought he would. A picnic with her family had sounded like the polar opposite of what he wanted from her. But he'd turned up, and her heart insisted on doing a Happy Dance at the thought of it, and the sight of him.

"Who wants to go in the water?" she asked, laughing at the chorus of "Me!" from the kids. They had a few extras along, as usual. And then it got even better, because Hemi stripped off the tank top to come join them, and Reka got a bit distracted.

Everything about him was perfect, and she remembered exactly why she'd danced with him, why she'd gone outside with him, why she'd gone to the hotel with him. The heavy bulge of shoulder muscle, the tapering vee of his torso, the horizontal ridges of his abdomen disappearing into the tops of his togs, which she didn't want to look at too closely. The slabs of his pectorals, one of them completely overlaid by the intricately curved lines of his moko, the Maori tattoo that extended over shoulder and arm, all the way to his elbow.

His pendant was a hei matau, a fish hook, she saw, rather than the toki, the adze she would have expected. She'd have thought it would have been all about strength and willpower.

Take the kids swimming, she reminded herself, so she did that, and he helped, not trying to talk to her, focusing on the kids, diving with them, swimming with them, giving them tosses through the air that had them shrieking and begging for more.

When they were back on shore again, and he was leaning back on an elbow on the blanket, still with that shirt off, his legs outstretched, eating a sandwich and seeming happy to be there with them, she gave in to temptation and looked her fill at his tattoo and his pendant—and the body they decorated.

He caught her looking and smiled, and she smiled back, because she couldn't help it.

"Why a fish hook?" she asked him.

Uncle Matiu answered before Hemi could. "Probably for safety over water. For good health and good luck. For the rugby."

"That's it," Hemi said, sitting up and nodding at her uncle with deference, holding the bit of carved greenstone in one of those clever hands, caressing its curves. "My dad gave it to me when I made the Under-19s. Letting me know that he believed I'd be traveling, that he believed I'd be doing this with my life. That he believed in me, I guess." He smiled, and it wasn't the cocky grin. It was sweet, real, and her heart melted a little.

"Where's your whanau, then, Hemi?" Auntie Kiri asked.

"The Far North," he answered. "Near Ahipara."

"Quite a distance from Auckland," Auntie Kiri commented. "Must get lonely."

Reka wanted to snort at that, because if there was one thing she was pretty sure Hemi wasn't, it was lonely.

To her surprise, though, he answered seriously, "It does. I asked my mum and dad about moving to Auckland, but they didn't want to leave, even though my sister and brother aren't there. They're both in Aussie, one in Queensland, one in Western Australia."

"That's where my man is," Ana put in, adjusting Tamati in her arms as she fed him, a nursing blanket draped over them for modesty. "Perth. For the mining. Wants us all to join him there, but I don't know. So far, and having my kids grow up Mozzies, it's hard. But we'll probably go all the same, because it's hard to be apart, too."

"Yeh. It is," Hemi said. "That's why my sister's there. Her man's in the mines as well. My brother's working construction on the Gold Coast. Good money, both of them, but you're right, far away. And a Maori Australian's still a Maori, but..." He sighed. "Not so much a Kiwi, eh. Anyway, I thought maybe my mum and dad wouldn't mind being closer to all of us, for holidays and such, visits. But it's the big whanau, I guess."

"Important," Uncle Matiu nodded. "Your own marae, your place, the cousins and aunties and uncles. When you get older, you appreciate it all more. That's what matters in the end, isn't it."

A short silence fell, broken by a small voice piping up from behind Reka where she sat, her legs tucked under her, on the blanket near—but not too near—Hemi.

"Sorry." It was Michael, seven years old, who'd been awestruck to see Hemi appear and had been hovering close ever since. He stood shifting from foot to foot with clear impatience, seizing his chance while the elders weren't talking. "Would you kick the footy with us?" He held the oval ball out, looked at Hemi imploringly. "Please?"

"Sweet as." Hemi got to his feet in one fluid, easy move, and the little gaggle of kids followed him down the beach as if he were the Pied Piper.

"Starstruck, that's what they are," Auntie Kiri said comfortably. "He's a pretty good bloke for all the celebrity, eh."

Reka shrugged. "Not too bad, I guess."

Ana looked across at her and laughed. "Not too bad? I don't call that not too bad."

Ella gave a sigh. "Yeh. You don't want him, Reka, I'll take him."

"Ian might not be too keen," Reka said.

"Yeh, well, a quick fling and no one the wiser, eh," Ella laughed back. "Maybe if I weren't quite so pregnant," she added, running a hand over the swell of her belly.

"That's what it would be, though." Reka was reminding herself as much as telling her cousins. "He's not interested. Not serious, I mean. He's just here because he's…" She glanced at Uncle Matiu. "Trying it on."

"Nah," he said. "I'm an old man now, but still a man, aren't I. A man doesn't turn up to meet your whanau if he's not interested, if he's not serious."

"Trust me, Uncle," she told him. "I know."

"Nah, you don't," he corrected her. "You assume. A man's a man, can't help that, but he's a person all the same. Give the boy a chance."

She'd already given him a chance, Reka thought uncomfortably. She'd given him more than that. That was the problem.

"*Tai!* Oh, my God! Tai!"

Everyone turned to stare at Ana. She was on her feet, still holding the nursing baby, frantically gesturing toward the sea.

Reka whirled and saw him. Her five-year-old nephew, head appearing briefly, one brown arm flung skyward, then disappearing under the waves again.

She didn't even know she was running until she hit the water. A few strides, and she had dived in and was swimming. Five fast strokes, six, into the deeper water, because the tide was high, and she was treading water, turning in a half-circle, but she couldn't see him.

She saw Hemi, though, powering through the waves a little farther out, to her right, and then she saw the little head again, and swam.

She reached Hemi as he got under Tai, lifted his head out of the water. The boy was gasping, choking, but breathing.

"Caught on something," Hemi told her urgently. "Can't tell what. Hold him. I'll dive down and see."

She took over from him, got Tai under the arms, his body hauled back against hers, her legs kicking hard to keep both of them afloat, as she felt whatever had caught the little boy trying to pull him down. She couldn't see Hemi below, couldn't focus on him anyway, not with Tai choking and coughing.

"Hang on, love," she told him. "We'll get you out."

Ana was in the water, she saw, and in another few seconds, she was there, too, face distraught, reaching for her boy, more hindrance than help.

But where was Hemi? The tugs Reka felt, threatening to pull Tai under, told her he was still there. But he had to come up soon. He had to.

Long seconds ticked by, and she had a sudden, irrational flash of panic that whatever it was under there had got Hemi, too, had pulled him down, and even as she was fighting the fear, he shot to the surface in a splash, heaving breath back into his lungs.

"Got fishing line wrapped around one foot," he got out through the gasps. "Can't pull it off by myself, line's too tight. I dove down to see if I could free it from whatever it's stuck on. No go."

He looked at Ana, who had her hands under Tai now. "Hold him for a minute," he told her. "Reka, I need you to dive with me, give me some slack on the line so I can work it off his foot."

"Got it," she said. She filled her lungs with air, saw him doing the same, and they dove together.

Luckily, the water was clear, and she could see. She obeyed Hemi's beckoning gesture, swam down below Tai's kicking foot, reached for the thin, translucent, painfully strong fishing line stretched taut beneath it, tugged up on it with all her might to give Hemi slack as he set to work to loosen it from around the boy's ankle. She didn't dare look to see if it was working, just held on, even as she felt the line slice into her hands from the force of her grip. The pain didn't register, just the desperate haste, and the message from her lungs.

As the seconds ticked by, she struggled with the attempt to hold her breath, and knew she was losing. It got worse and worse, until she had to breathe. She *had* to.

At last, she couldn't hold on any more. She shot to the surface, heaved in a few gasping lungsful of breath, didn't answer Ana's frantic question, and dove again. No choice.

winning effort

♡

Hemi had felt the moment when Reka had let go of the line, had fought to maintain the precious progress he'd made. He had managed to work the barely-visible snare most of the way over Tai's heel, and he held it in place grimly until she returned, then set to his task again. He was getting a bit lightheaded now, but he wasn't giving up.

He forced his mind into the calm place he went when he kicked. A crowd of eighty thousand in Twickenham Stadium, though, roaring and stomping out their attempt to distract him from a final-seconds, match-winning penalty kick, couldn't hold a candle to this. Because this was a life, a child's life.

He held his breath, and he stayed patient, and he worked, and Reka held on beneath him, giving him the slack he needed, and, at last, the heel was clear and he was able to shove the line the last few desperate centimeters over the boy's foot. And Tai was free.

The instant he saw the little body bobbing up like a cork, he grabbed for Reka, aimed for an arm and caught her hair instead, the braid floating above her, and hauled her by it to the surface, shoved her up before surfacing himself, where he heaved and gasped and felt the precious oxygen returning to his depleted lungs, unable to do anything else for a full minute.

When he could focus again, he saw Ana struggling towards shore with the boy, swam to help her as Reka, who had been gasping beside him, did the same. Hemi took the boy from his floundering mother, saw Reka reaching for her cousin, talking to her, helping her, and he put an arm across Tai's chest, got on his back with the boy, holding him tight.

"Kia kaha, little bro," he told him. He sensed Tai's struggles easing as he tried to obey, as he tried to be strong, and felt a flash of admiration for his courage even through the residue of fear and adrenaline.

He side-stroked to shore like that, his body knowing exactly what to do, stood when he felt the touch of the sandy bottom against one foot, swept Tai into his arms and ran with him to the blanket, set him down in the midst of his anxious family.

The boy was all right, he saw with relief. Eyes wide, crying a bit, but excited, too, the little bugger.

He ran back down into the water to help Reka, who was supporting a weeping Ana up onto the beach.

"No worries," he told the sobbing mother, wrapping his own arm around her and half-carrying her to join her son. "It's all good. He's had another adventure, lived to tell the tale."

No lasting harm done to anyone, in fact. Except that it might have taken a few years off his own life, and Reka's and Ana's, too.

"I'm sorry," he had to say as the family made hasty preparations to depart. "That I didn't see him go in the water. We were kicking, and I just...I missed it."

"Not your fault," Uncle Matiu said. "Our fault. Somebody needs to be watching the kids all the time near water. We forgot that. We all did. We won't forget it again."

Ana nodded, holding her baby to her in one arm, her son cuddled close with the other, looking drained. The tears were still trickling, and Hemi could tell that her mind was going over and over the sequence of events, imagining the worst and suffering with it.

"Come on, love," Kiri urged her stricken daughter. "I'll go home with you, look after the kids, fix you a cuppa, let you have a lie-down. Soon be better."

Hemi helped Reka pack up blankets, towels, the remains of their picnic, threw a bag over one shoulder and supported Ana up the path to the cars. Kiri got behind the wheel with Ana and three of the kids, while Ella situated Uncle Matiu in the front of the other car and loaded up the back with five more kids, which involved some double-buckling of seatbelts and was probably, Hemi thought, making everybody think twice. Nothing like a near-miss to highlight the risks.

He shoved the picnic bags into the boot, slammed it shut again, looked at Reka. "No room, eh."

"No." She still looked shaken herself, and no wonder. "I walked."

"Walk you back, then," he suggested.

She nodded, and they watched the cars depart, then set off up the hill in their wake.

"I just—" Reka began. "I was so scared. Now I'm thinking, why didn't I swim back for a knife?"

"Did anyone have a knife?"

"Uncle Matiu will have had. But I didn't think."

"Hard to think, in the middle of it. For anyone."

"*You* were thinking. You knew what to do."

"Because I'm used to thinking under pressure, making decisions fast, backing myself," he tried to explain. "That's the job. That's being a first-five all over. You just get into the zone and focus. And the adrenaline helps, too."

She nodded again, shifted her grip on her bag as they stepped onto the footpath leading through the Domain, and he saw her wince. He took the thing off her shoulder, put it on his own, then stopped. "Let's see your hands," he said.

She lifted her palms, and they both looked at the slices across them, the cuts lacing the sensitive flesh of her fingers.

"Hurts, eh," he said.

"Yeh." She laughed a little. "Didn't even feel it, at the time. Guess you know about that, too."

"I do." He frowned at the red lines. "We'll put something on that," he decided. "Got some stuff back at your place, or do we need to pop into a shop on the way?"

"Think I've got it," she said.

They started walking again, and he let her talk it out, understanding the need to rehash, to relive the experience, to reassure herself that it had all turned out all right. And when they got to her house, he went in with her, up the stairs and through to her tiny granny flat around the back.

She hesitated, though, in the lounge. "I want a shower," she said, feeling her braid, what he knew was the salt-stickiness of it. "Otherwise, I'll have to do it all over, the bandaging and that."

"I'll wait here for you then, shall I?" he asked.

She stood a moment, and he found himself holding his breath again, for an entirely different reason this time.

"Yeh," she finally said. "If you don't mind. I could use the help. So hard to do your own hands."

He sat and waited, and then, when she came out again, wearing the green skirt, her hair back in its knot, he followed her into the little bathroom, took the ointment and plasters, and doctored up her hands as best he could. Stood close beside her, holding one hand at a time and dabbing the cuts gently with ointment, feeling her trying not to wince, and completely aware of her presence. It was more than the heat, now, though that was still there, too, pulling him towards her like a magnet, the electricity of the contact powerful, and all he was doing was holding her hand in his own.

"There," he said when he finished, sweeping the rubbish into the bin. "You'll do, now."

"Thanks," she said.

"Can I…" He hesitated. "D'you have to work tonight, or could we have dinner? Just dinner," he went on hastily. "I promise."

"I'd like to have dinner," she said. "But going out, everyone seeing us…"

"Tell you what," he decided. "I'll do a bit of fishing, see if I can catch something for our tea. We'll go back to the Domain and have a barbecue. No pressure. Just dinner and a chat."

She smiled, and he could see the teasing light back in her eyes, her spirits rallying. "What if you don't catch anything? Bit of a knock to the pride, eh."

He laughed back at her. "Then I go to the shop, take the paper off, and tell you I caught it. No worries. You'll get fish."

"I'll bring a salad," she decided.

"Perfect. Walking OK, or do you want to drive?"

"Walking's good."

"I'll collect you around seven, then, how's that?"
She smiled again. "It's a date."

♡

He did catch a snapper, to his relief. Whatever he'd said, it had mattered. He walked with her, ten short minutes to the Domain, their earlier journey in reverse, everything easier between them now, lighter. Tai was back to normal, she'd told him, the adults suffering far more repercussions than the boy had from his close call.

"What did you do this afternoon?" he asked her when he'd set the bags down on a picnic table near a barbecue.

"Had a rest," she admitted. "Felt good."

"Day off today, then?" he asked, pulling the bottle of chilled Sauvignon Blanc out of the bag of supplies he'd picked up at Four Square, twisting off the lid and pouring wine into the plastic glasses.

"Not the poshest," he said, handing one to her, "but the wine should be all right."

"Cheers." She touched her glass to his, and he remembered their first drink of champagne together, and could tell from the arrested look in her eyes that she did, too.

"Yeh," she said, then elaborated at his confused look. "Day off, I mean. I'm just filling in at a couple places right now, making a bit extra during the school holidays."

"During the holidays," he said slowly. "Are you a student, then?" He had no idea, he realized, what she did for work. He'd assumed it was the waitress thing.

"No, a teacher. A kindy teacher." She caught his startled look and smiled. "Surprised you, didn't I? Not how kindy teachers are meant to behave, is it?"

"Oh, I don't know," he said, taking another sip of wine and grinning at her. "I'd say you're exactly the kind of kindy teacher I like best. You do that here in Russell, or someplace else?"

"Here," she said. "I teach here. I went away to Uni, but I came back, because Northland is home."

♡

"What did you mean," she asked him when they were sitting backwards on the picnic bench next to each other, legs outstretched, dinner eaten, finishing off the bottle, "when you said it was different now? Different from a year ago? Because you are a bit different, aren't you?"

He looked up at the sky, beginning to darken into dusk now, and thought about it. "Reckon I am," he said. "Although at the time I said that, I'm not sure I knew what I meant."

"Because at the time you said it, which was all of yesterday, you were trying it on."

"Well, yeh." He flashed a smile her way. "Still am, come to that. If we're being honest here, and I think that's the point, eh."

"Yeh," she said. "That's the point."

"But last year," he went on, wanting to explain it to her, "it was all new. It was all...overwhelming. Being selected, calling my family to tell them. Training with the All Blacks, thinking I'd be sitting in the reserves, just getting a taste of it. And then having to go on after all, having to start, when JT pulled his hamstring at the Captain's Run. All of a sudden, there I was, in the spotlight, against France of all people, directing the boys round the park."

"But you did so well," she said. "Everyone said you did so well."

"I was nervy, though," he admitted. "That whole end-of-year tour was a blur. Everything was so new, and so exciting. The pressure, not wanting to make a hash of it. I was good once I got on the paddock, but before, and afterwards…" He exhaled. "It was a bit hard."

"So you consoled yourself."

"Well, yeh, I did. Because that was new, too," he tried to explain. "I mean, when you play footy, the girls are interested anyway, but I guess you know that."

"I saw that," she said. "At the wedding."

"Because I was an All Black, then. And it felt good. It felt good for a long time, feeling like I could have whatever I wanted. Whoever I wanted." He stopped. "Sorry. Guess that was a bit too honest."

"No," she said. "Hard to hear, but still good. Honest is good, and I knew that anyway, so having you say it lets me know you're telling the truth, that's all."

He nodded, so grateful that he hadn't stuffed up utterly, and kept on. "This year, though, it started being a bit different. I started getting the feeling, is it me they want? Or is it me, the footy player? Or is it even worse, just shagging an All Black, and any one would do? And I started realizing that every girl wasn't the same. And I'm sorry I didn't call," he managed to say, because he knew he had to say it, "but I got caught up in it all again. I meant to, I meant to ring you straight away, but it was exciting, and we were training, and then traveling, and I…I guess I wasn't ready to admit that it might have meant something after all, until I saw you again."

"So you've changed, that what you're telling me?" she asked, and he could see the little smile hovering around the corners of her mouth.

"Maybe. Not changed so much yet, maybe," he said, throwing his hat fully into the ring, because it wasn't going to work with her, he could tell, unless he really did tell her the truth. "But I think I'm ready to. I think I want to."

"But can you?" she asked. "Can you really?"

"I can do most things I've tried," he said, because that was true too. "When I want to. And I want to, with you. I want to do this. I know we didn't start right, not that I'm sorry. I could tell you I was, but it'd be a lie, because I'm not a bit sorry. I'd only be sorry if we didn't get to do it again. But I know we did it in the wrong order. Had the sex first, and now we need to go back and get the romance."

"That what you want, then?" she asked, and the smile was there, but she was serious, too, he could tell. "The romance?"

"Well, I want the sex, too," he admitted, and he was laughing back at her. "I want both. Can I get both? That an option?"

"Not tonight, it's not," she said. "Not with you going back to Auckland tomorrow. But you could kiss me, don't you think?"

So he did. He scooted a bit closer to her on the wooden bench, smiled into her eyes in the soft twilight, put a gentle hand on the side of her face, felt her leaning into his palm as if she needed his touch as much as he needed hers.

He bent his head and touched his lips to hers, and the electricity was back, every nerve ending tingling as he continued to kiss her, long and slow and so sweet. His hand stroking over her cheek, his other arm going around her waist, because that was his spot, that deep indentation. That was where he was meant to hold Reka.

Her bandaged hands came up to his shoulders, and she hung on and kissed him back, faint sounds coming from the mouth he held beneath his own, sounds of desire and longing and needing. To go further, to have it all, to take everything he wanted to give her. He knew what she was feeling, because he was feeling it, too. And when he dragged his lips from her mouth and began to kiss her neck, the sounds weren't quite so muffled, and she was squirming a little on the bench, and he wanted her so much, it was hurting now.

In the end, he was the one who pulled back. He gave her one last soft kiss on the mouth, rested his forehead against hers, closed his eyes, and sighed.

"Need to stop," he said. "If we're only doing the romance tonight, we need to stop."

She laughed a little, a breathy, unsteady sound that wasn't Reka at all. "Yeh. Romance, not sex. Because you're leaving tomorrow."

"But I'm coming back," he told her, not letting go of her yet, because he couldn't.

"Are you?" she asked, and she wasn't laughing now.

"I am. Just for you."

♡

He walked her home in the slowly deepening dusk of a Northland summer, held her hand—carefully, gently, because she could tell he knew it still hurt, and his care made her melt a little bit more inside. Her body was at once charged, electric with the tingling energy of being kissed and touched by Hemi, and deliciously fatigued. She wasn't satisfied, she wasn't even close. She was right up in the air, trembling with it. But she felt *good.*

"Home," he said when they got there, and she could hear his reluctance to be there. He pulled her into the shadows at the side of the house, and it was like that first time, but so unlike it, too. He plunged both hands in her hair, cupping her head, and lifted her face to his, then bent to kiss her again.

He started out gentle, but when she had her hands on his shoulders, was pressed up against him, it changed fast. His mouth was moving over hers, his hands grasping her head with the same urgency that was sending her hands of their own accord down his arms to stroke the hard swell of bicep, the secret, velvety softness of the skin of his inner arms, and she could feel how much he liked having her touch him, having her want him.

"Aw, Reka," he sighed, lifting his mouth from hers at last and stepping back a reluctant pace. "I want to take you to bed so badly. And you want it too, don't you?"

"Yeh," she said unsteadily. "I do. You know I do. But not tonight. Later. If you come back."

"*When* I come back."

He dropped his hands, then, and she gathered the final tiny shreds of self-control left to her and walked away from him, feeling his eyes on her as surely as his hands and mouth had been.

But if there were ever going to be more than sex between them, they had to see what that was, and they had to let it grow. She knew it. So she walked away.

♡

Hemi watched her go inside, and ached for her. He thought about going back to his room, or going for a beer, and rejected both ideas.

Instead, he walked. It was nearly fully dark now, and he soon left the streetlights behind as he turned up the road, climbing the hill that rose above Tapeka Point.

It didn't take long to reach the top, and luckily, the moon was nearly full tonight, lighting his way. He walked to the edge, looked out over the dark murmur below that was the sea, out and up to the pinpricks of light that had begun to appear, the impossible, incredible multitude of stars just starting to be visible, reminding him of home, far from the light of the cities. The land, the sky, the sea, and the stars. The North.

He stood, raised his arms slowly overhead until his hands reached toward those points of light, felt his feet rooting down, connecting to this place, and let the intention, the purpose fill him.

I'm coming back.

He told the sky above him, and he told the earth below him. He told Reka, and he told himself.

I'm coming back.

promises kept

♡

An endless two weeks later, and she was beginning to realize that this was going to be even harder than she'd thought.

He'd gone back to Auckland for a mere ten days, then had been off to Sydney for a preseason match against the Waratahs that the Blues had lost. When she'd texted him her commiserations afterwards, though, he'd told her it didn't matter.

Preseason doesn't count, he'd texted back. *Just trying the boys out.*

She guessed it made sense, because he'd played a bare fifteen minutes himself, although he told her he'd wanted more.

"I always want to be out on the park," he said when he rang her from the airport the next morning. "All the time. Every match. Most of us do."

"But...aren't you worried you'll be injured before the season even starts? That must be what the coaches are thinking about." She curled onto the couch, held her phone to her ear and wished she were holding him, but was happy just to hear his voice.

She could almost hear the shrug. "You can always get injured. Can get injured in training, can't you. Strain a groin muscle, kicking over and over again to get it right, and you've lost weeks of playing time. Besides, match time is different to training time. The pace, the pressure."

"Thought preseason didn't matter," she challenged.

She got a laugh in return. "All right. It all matters. Anytime you play, anything you play, you want to win. If you don't burn to win, you aren't meant for this game."

Was that all it was about, then, with her? she wondered. Winning? But they weren't talking about her, and she bit her tongue on the question. Needy didn't suit her.

"I'm coming to see you after this next one," he told her as if he could read her thoughts. "What time do you get off work on Monday?"

"Four." He was coming, and the happiness fizzed inside her like bubbles in a Coke bottle. He was coming back.

"Unless you want me sooner," he said, and she heard the hint of laughter in his voice. "I'd get a late start, for obvious reasons, and I wouldn't get there till late on Sunday, but I'm willing to put in the hard yards. Be able to stay up late with you then, keep you…company."

"Monday," she said, her smile huge. "Because I want you fit and rested for me. But don't get your hopes up."

"Aw, baby," he said, "a man can always hope," and she laughed.

♡

The second game of the preseason, the Crusaders this time. A New Zealand derby, North versus South, and Reka was in the Duke on another Saturday night, the room buzzing once more with noise and laughter. Locals and holiday-makers both, the perfect February weather bringing no lessening of crowds here in the perpetual summer of the Bay of Islands.

She wasn't serving tonight, though, because she wanted to watch Hemi. She waited impatiently through the first half at the big round table she'd got here early to secure, but he didn't appear.

Everyone was here with her, as usual. Uncle Matiu, Auntie Kiri, Ana and Ella and a couple more cousins. Tamati sleeping in his carrier against the wall, Tai and the other kids busy scoffing chips and sausages, content for now. Nobody paying much attention to the game except herself and Uncle Matiu.

Reka forgot about the rest of them, though, when the adverts for DIY projects and manufactured homes, preventatives against parasites and Dry Cow Mastitis, and all the rest of the inevitable accompaniment to a New Zealand rugby match had played out, and half-time was over. Her attention was all for the big screen overhead, because Hemi was filling it, running onto the field for the kickoff in his tight blue jersey and little shorts, his hair cut close and crisp, every bit of his big body looking rock-hard and ready for action, like he couldn't wait, and just looking at him like that made her shiver.

He gave the ball a quick bounce and sent it off his toe in a high punt aimed perfectly just the required twenty-two meters down the field and barely inside the touchline, forcing the men in red to waste time positioning them-selves and allowing the Blues to sprint down and chal-lenge for the ball, and the second half was underway.

It wasn't all perfect, not at all. More than one pass went awry, more than one player was left grasping air as his opponent swerved out of his tackle.

"Dead sloppy," Uncle Matiu said. "Off pace, both teams. Not clicking at all. They'll need to get that sorted, specially the Blues, if they want to finish anywhere in the top half of the pack this year."

Reka wasn't listening, because the huge Crusaders lock carrying the ball had just charged at Hemi, thinking that a 10 would be a soft target, and Hemi had taken him on. She winced at the collision even as her heart swelled with pride at his courage.

The Blues' massive No. 8, Finn Douglas, was there immediately in support, shoving against the Crusaders players who'd joined the breakdown to fight for the ball, and Drew Callahan, the Blues' captain, was in there digging as well, going for the steal.

"Nothing wrong with their ticker, though," Uncle Matiu said, and Reka agreed, but the next moment, she was leaping to her feet. Her eyes had never left Hemi, and it looked to her like somehow, he had the ball.

In the same instant, though, a player in a red shirt was coming across, reaching desperately to try to get it back. Hemi rolled, the arriving player's knee caught him in the head, and Reka was still up, hands clasped at her chest, forgetting to breathe.

The referee blew his whistle to signal the change of possession and the teams set up again, a Blues player running with the ball, passing it a split-second before the arriving tackler took him down, but Reka wasn't watching that. She was looking for Hemi.

A pan back downfield by one of the cameras, and there he was, still on the ground, the trainer bent over him with his black bag at the ready. Hemi was rolling, though, up on one knee, then getting to his feet, running back to join the play, and Reka tried to catch her breath as the camera showed a quick replay of the collision and the crowd voiced its noisy disapproval.

To no effect, because Hemi was straight back in the mix, carrying the ball now, powering forward off his muscular legs and taking a couple Crusaders with him before going down again, and Reka was sitting down and patting her chest.

"Got a hard head, hasn't he," Uncle Matiu said with a wheezy chuckle, and Reka turned to glare at him.

"That wasn't right," she said. "Kneeing him in the head."

"That's the game, my darling. That's what he'd tell you. That's the game."

Hemi didn't play the full forty minutes for all that, she saw with some relief. Seventy minutes in, and he was jogging to the sideline to applause from the crowd, accepting slaps on the back from his teammates on the bench—and then accepting a blue ice bag, sitting down and pressing it to his jaw, turning to his neighbor all the same for a smile and a quick word. Not fussed at all, Uncle Matiu had been right about that.

"A man who can do that," she asked her uncle as the camera shifted back to the match, which the Blues seemed to be winning, "who can play that hard, be that fierce, get hurt like that and keep playing, that says heaps about him, doesn't it?"

"Says he's brave," Uncle Matiu said. "But you knew that already. You saw him save Tai. You don't need to watch him play rugby to know he's strong and brave. That isn't the part that counts most anyway."

"It isn't?" It counted to her.

"Nah," he said with decision, lifting his beer to his lips with one leathery brown hand and taking a sip. He set the handle down, wiped his mouth, and Reka waited. What counted, if that didn't?

"That he was *able* to save Tai, that isn't the point," her uncle continued at last. "Just like you were able to do it, because you're a good swimmer too. You were able to, and you got stuck in and did it, because Tai's your nephew, he's your blood. But he isn't Hemi's. Strong is one thing. Brave is one thing. Heaps of war heroes who're rubbish at home, though. What matters..." He thumped his skinny old-man's chest. "Mana. That's what matters. That he runs strongly, that he fights bravely, yeh. And that he can speak softly, that he uses his strength to protect, not just to hurt. That's what you know about him. That's what counts."

♡

A day and a half later, she was still waiting for him, and her kids seemed to have got together and determined to make her life difficult. All she wanted was for the work day to be over, to go home and get ready for Hemi, and she could swear they knew it.

She sniffed as she approached the little group at the corner table. Oh, bugger. She knew what that was. They had been happily coloring just a minute before, but there was some shrieking going on now.

"Ewww!" Mandy exclaimed, her voice shrill with excitement, brown ponytail bobbing as she jumped up. "Somebody has pee-pee pants!"

"Robby!" Beauden shouted. "Robby weed in his pants!"

Robby had stopped coloring and started to cry, rocking a little in his little wooden chair.

"He's a crybaby!" Beauden said. "Robby weed in his pants, and he's crying, because he's a baby!"

"He's a big baby," Mandy echoed. "Robby's a big, big baby."

"Stop it," Reka said firmly, gathering Robby off his chair, the telltale acrid aroma letting her know that Beauden had pinpointed the sufferer. "Just about everybody in this room has weed in their pants at school, and you all know it. Today's Robby's turn, that's all."

"I didn't," Mandy said stoutly. "I *never* did."

"You spewed, though," Beauden said with delight. "I remember. You got sick all over the doll corner! Miss Reka had to clean it all up!"

"Everybody has accidents," Reka said, trying not to sigh. "Every single one of us. Stop crying, Robby. Let's get your clean pants." She nodded across the room to Heather, her aide, took Robby by the hand, and set off for his cubby as the little boy wiped a hand under his running nose, still sniffling. Geez. Mondays.

A half-hour later, she had the kids on the round carpet in the center of the room, singing the alphabet song. Calm and structure, she'd decided. Wouldn't do her any harm either.

A sudden outbreak of four-year-old giggles, then a pair of strong brown legs at the edge of her vision, and that wasn't something you saw much of in her classroom. She turned her head, and her voice trailed off. A few of the kids were still singing, plowing on to the end, and then they were all staring and giggling.

Hemi. Standing next to the bricks table, a grin on his face, an enormous bouquet of orange Asiatic lilies in his arms. Shorts, jandals, blue T-shirt stretching across that broad chest. Hemi. With a jaw darkened and swollen with bruising, and she exclaimed aloud at the sight of it as she got to her feet, but he paid that no attention.

"Hi," he said. "Decided I couldn't wait another minute to see my favorite kindy teacher."

Heather came over with a smile on her round face, gave Reka a little dig in the ribs, and eased her middle-aged body down to the carpet to take her place. "Come on, kids," she said. "Zippety-zap! Get ready to wiggle your body!"

Reka barely heard the group starting to sing behind her, because Hemi had put his arms around her, flowers and all. He was holding her, and she was holding him back, loving that she was in his arms again, wishing he would kiss her but knowing it would hurt, and the kids weren't zippety-zapping nearly as much as they ought to have been.

"Whoa, boy," she said when she was finally able to get herself under control and step back. She took the flowers from him, laughing and heated and so happy to see him. "You really know how to turn an impressionable girl's head."

"That's what I'm hoping." He watched, his smile lopsided, painful, probably, but broad all the same, as she buried her nose in the extravagantly scented mass. "Believe me, that's what I'm hoping."

That wasn't the only surprise he had in store, she discovered a couple hours later when he came to collect her at her flat.

"Lucky it's summer," he said, eyeing her yellow sundress with approval.

"Why's that?" She laughed again, because she couldn't help laughing, because she was walking down the Chapel Street hill with him holding her hand.

"Well, because you're not wearing much, for one thing. But also because we've got enough light left for this."

"For what, exactly?" All he'd told her was to pack her togs and towel, and she'd been surprised when he'd headed in the exact wrong direction for the beach.

He took her across the minimal traffic on The Strand, through the line of ancient trees stretching along the shore beside the harbor, onto the jetty leading to the little platform that was Russell Wharf, and nodded at the sleek white power boat moored there. "For me to impress you," he told her. "As much as I can right now, anyway. At least I hope so."

"We going out in Ewan's boat?" she asked with pleasure. A bit above her touch. If she needed to go somewhere, the ferry or an occasional water taxi was as flash as she got.

"We are," he said, his hand around hers as he handed her down into it, then jumped down himself with their bags, stowed them at the direction of the man waiting for them, his face and arms seamed and brown from a lifetime on the water.

"Afternoon, Reka," Ewan said. "This fella come back for you, did he?" Because of course Ewan knew her business. Everybody did.

"Where are we going?" Reka asked, deciding not to answer him.

"It's a surprise," Hemi said, and Ewan smiled at Reka, closed one brown eye in a slow wink.

It didn't take her long to suss it out, of course, not when the boat rounded the end of the peninsula, headed northeast, and the broad, scooped bay of Motuarohia Island came into view. Barely twenty minutes later, because Ewan's flash boat had a pretty powerful motor.

A few sailboats bobbed at their moorings, a few afternoon visitors walked the beach, and otherwise, there was nothing but bush, sand, and bright blue sea. Ewan loaded the two of them into the dinghy along with a chilly bin and a bag of snorkel equipment, and Reka laughed again.

"You really have done it up right," she told Hemi.

"Hope so," he said.

Ewan piloted the little dinghy up onto the sand and Reka jumped out, sandals in hand, into the bit of surf near shore, the hem of her sundress catching a bit of salt water along the way, but who cared about that?

"Two hours," Ewan told Hemi before taking himself off to the boat again.

"You can't snorkel, though," Reka objected once Hemi had carried their chilly bin and gear up the beach, set them near a gnarled old tree growing sideways at the edge of the sand. "Not with your face."

He looked at her in surprise. "Course I can."

"But won't it hurt?"

He shrugged. "It hurts anyway. May as well do something I like. You want to make me feel better, I can still flag Ewan down. I don't mind turning straight around again. Not at all."

She laughed. "Nah, boy. I'm not that easy anymore, remember? Takes more than flowers and a boat ride, much as I love that you did them both. Let's walk to the top first, though. I love the view from here."

"Suits me," he said, and they left their gear where it was, climbed the half-kilometer track up through the bush.

She followed Hemi up. No habitations here, nobody but the occasional boatie, nothing but sea and sand, ferns and native hardwoods and the ever-present gnarled trunks of pohutukawa, their red blossoms fallen to the ground now, but the berries attracting the tui and bellbirds whose musical calls filled the air. A breeze stirred the long fronds of the fern trees to either side, and a cheeky little fantail swooped and darted around them, aiming for the insects stirred up by the humans' passing feet.

Reka inhaled the joy of being here. Of walking with Hemi, of following his broad back, his sturdy brown legs as they planted themselves in the earth, making short work of the little climb. No matter that his body, as well as his face, had to still be aching and sore.

They paused at the top, turned three hundred and sixty degrees to take in the view, and her heart sang.

The Bay of Islands expanded before them in every direction, endless blue water punctuated by the irregular shapes of islands colored all the variegated greens of the Northland bush. The peninsula that held Russell stretched out long to the southwest, a larger smear of green, but the tiny settlement was invisible from where they stood, and it was as if nobody else existed, as if the two of them were alone in this pristine world.

He reached for her from behind, and she relaxed back against his chest, felt his arms wrap around her.

"Looks just the way it must have when the ancestors came," he said, and she hummed her reply.

They stood like that, looking out, Hemi strong and solid behind her, content just to hold her, and she was happy.

"This is the best part of my week," he said after a moment. "Coming here."

She laughed a little. "Considering the other part of your week was getting bashed in the head, not sure that's too flattering."

She felt the rumble of his own laugh radiate through her. "Even so, baby. Even so."

"You won, anyway."

"Yeh, it was nice, but it's what I told you. Preseason."

"You looked good, though," she insisted. "You looked so good. Even after you did get bashed in the head."

He shrugged, she felt it. "That's the job."

She laughed a bit more, and he said, "What?"

"That's what my Uncle Matiu said. Exactly that. That's what he said you would say."

"He's a wise old one, eh."

"He is."

Hemi hesitated a moment. "I've met a fair bit of your whanau now. But never your own mum and dad, your brothers and sisters. Thought you were from Russell."

"Ah," she said. "My dad buggered off to Aussie a long time ago, that's why. Got some other kids, across the Ditch."

"Oh. Sorry."

"Nah. It happens. What men do."

"Some men," he said, his voice quiet. "Some men."

"Yeh. Men like him."

"And your mum?"

"Oh, she's around. Down in Whangarei now, though, working there."

"Mmm. Not much work in the North."

"No," she said on a sigh. "There isn't. That's why I'm a kindy teacher. There'll always be kids, as long as there are people."

"At least as long as some of those people are Maori," he said, and she laughed again.

♡

They headed back down the track again after a few more minutes, got their gear on and cooled their heated bodies in the crystalline waters of the sweeping bay, the sea glowing an unearthly turquoise in the slowly fading light of a Northland summer evening, and it was even better, swimming slowly with Hemi and looking at the world beneath. The spiky black of kina, the multicolored sea stars near the shore, and then, farther out, the red moki, the gorgeous blue of a maomao darting by, the silver flash of the black-striped parore. And the mighty snapper, as much as a meter long, making their majestic way through the kelp beds.

They sat on their twisting branch afterwards, sedate in the view of the boats at anchor around them, and ate their picnic. Nothing flash, sandwiches and another bottle of white wine drunk from plastic glasses. Perfect. And then Ewan was buzzing toward shore in the little dinghy and their lazy evening was coming to an end.

"Too short," she sighed, tossing the last of the rubbish into the chilly bin and closing the lid.

"And I have training in the morning," he said. "Too short. But good, eh."

"Yeh." She smiled at him, put a gentle hand on the uninjured side of his jaw, and gave him a soft kiss there. "So good."

♡

"Have a good time?" Ewan asked them when they were back on the boat and underway again, to Hemi's regret.

"Brilliant," Reka said, and he glowed a little inside.

"Other than that she outswam me," he told the older man. "Got a glimpse of an eagle ray, and off she went. Couldn't keep up. My ego's still smarting."

Ewan laughed. "She'll do that. Been a surf lifesaver from the time she was about fifteen, eh."

"Fourteen," she said, and Hemi saw her wicked smile at the expression on his face and had to smile himself.

"Well, I know she's not bad at lifesaving," he said.

"Not so bad yourself, are you," she answered.

"Our women's team took second place in the Northland Surf Lifesaving Challenge not so long ago," Ewan went on, chatty now. "We were pretty chuffed about that. With Reka, of course. I wouldn't be too quick to take her on in a paddling contest either, unless you're sure you've got the bollocks for it."

"The bollocks to lose, you mean," Hemi said.

Ewan had a good laugh about that. "Yeh. Think you're man enough for her? I'd say it'd take a fair bit of confidence."

"I guess she'll be the judge of that, eh, Reka."

"Yeh." She was laughing now too. "If you're not well and truly warned off by now, and you want to have a go, I'm willing."

"Works for me," Hemi said, and Ewan just smiled.

The boat picked up speed, out on the open water, and he saw her shiver a little. He wrapped an arm around her, pulled her up against his side, felt her snuggle up closer, and sighed himself, because that was good.

He would have helped her out of the boat, too, but she didn't need his help. As soon as Ewan had eased the craft into the tiny landing stage that was Russell Wharf and tied off, she was grabbing her bag, jumping down onto the dock with a "Cheers" for the skipper, and Hemi was left with nothing to do but follow her.

"So," he said. He took her bag from her, because that was one thing he was going to do no matter what. He slung it onto his shoulder, then took her hand and threaded his fingers through hers. "Any chance of you sending me on my way back to training tomorrow with a smile on my face?"

She was nestled up close again, but didn't answer for a moment.

"I want you to know," she finally said as they began the steep climb up Chapel Street past the church, past the ancient graves of soldiers and sailors killed in the skirmishes for this ground, the white headstones ghostly in the starlight. "It's not just...I'm not playing. This isn't some game, some hoop I'm trying to make you jump through. It's that I'm afraid I like you too much, and I don't know you well enough, to risk it. To risk my heart. Not with everything you are, everything that's out there for you."

"And everything you know about me," he said, and wished it weren't true. "Not the way you risked it last time, because I broke it. I know I did. I thought we both knew we were having fun. I thought that was all I was having, and that it was enough."

"Well, to be fair, I'm not even sure you broke my heart," she said, and surely only Reka would be that honest. "More my pride, maybe. But now..."

"Yeh," he said. "Different for me too. And I know. I know it's your heart, now. And it matters to me, your heart."

"It does? You sure about that?"

He smiled and kept walking. As steep as the incline was, she wasn't out of breath, just as she hadn't been on the island. "Yeh. Because I'm selfish about it. I want you to give it to me. And when you do, I want all of it, so it would be better for me if it were whole, eh."

He could hear her sigh. They had turned her corner now, and unfortunately, had reached her front door, and this was where he drove away and left her again. The velvety dusk had turned to full, black night, uninterrupted by anything as prosaic as street lighting, and he wouldn't have been able to see her at all if the night hadn't been so clear, if the stars hadn't been so spectacular, complete with the broad, bright streak that was the Milky Way.

He turned, took her in his arms, and felt the way she came to him. He didn't kiss her, but she kissed him again, the gentlest press of her lips against the aching soreness that, for all its throbbing insistence, was no match for the way the rest of his body ached for her.

She clung to him a moment, then pulled back. "So hard, when it's so good."

"I did all right, then," he said. "Made you happy."

"Yeh. You did. I think you'd better get on back to Auckland, though, before I forget myself and ask you to make me happier."

He smiled. "I'll do that. And I'll work out how to see you again, soon as we can manage it. We'll get to work on that heart of yours."

He was almost to his car when he turned around and said, his voice not loud but carrying across to her all the same, "Think about me."

"That's all?" she called softly back. "Just think?"

"Well, watch me, too, if you get the chance of it. Watch me, and know that I will've been thinking about you too. You can count on that."

sex, sport, and rock & roll

♡

"Nah, I dunno," Hemi said on the following Saturday night, reaching into his locker for his shirt, pulling it over his chest and tugging it down, wincing inwardly now that the adrenaline was no longer coursing through his body, leaving him with the throbbing reminder of every single tackle he'd made and received over the past couple hours.

"Why not?" Aaron asked, lifting his foot to the bench to lace his shoe. "It's going to be an awesome night. Best one yet. Damn, I'm good at this. I should go into business. Party planning." He chuckled.

"Yeh, well," Hemi said. "There's a word for that."

"You saying I'm a pimp?" Aaron laughed again. "Could be, mate. Could be. Wait till you see Mandy. Let's say she's got some talents her parents probably don't know about, and a fair few friends who are as hot as she is—and just about as inhibited. She told me the Blues are their very favorite team, and you know how those girls love to support the team. Heaps of the other boys are coming. We got the win, time to celebrate."

"In preseason," Hemi pointed out. "Which means just about nothing."

"You get religion, these past weeks? No fun at all, are you. Is it that girl? The one in Russell?"

"Yeh," Hemi said. "Maybe it is. Or could be it's all just getting a bit old."

"A bit *old?*" Aaron asked in astonishment. "What, footy, beer, sex? Yeh, some of my least favorite things, aren't they. You're whipped, is what it is. A couple days with one girl, and I've lost my wingman."

"I'm not your wingman." Hemi got his own shoes on and started to pack up his kit.

"All right," Aaron said. "I'm *your* wingman. I've lost my…wingmaster." He laughed again, because seriousness wasn't Aaron's strong suit. "Come on. You can spend the night staring disapprovingly at the rest of us if you like, while we take advantage of what's on offer. But I told Mandy you'd be there, and she's got a couple of friends who're dying to meet you. You'll ruin my party before it starts if you aren't there. Don't let me down, I'm begging you, because that girl's got a mouth like a hoover."

"Aw, that's some class," Hemi said.

"Come on," Aaron urged. "Help a mate out. What are you going to do otherwise?"

"Dunno. Early night?" At Aaron's snort, he added piously, "My body is a temple."

"Yeh, right. A temple you could find a girl or two to worship at tonight. I know that's my plan. Come on. It'll be good. You'll see."

Aaron was right, Hemi decided. Where was the harm? It was just a party. No harm in going to a party. Not like he had anything else to do.

♡

It was, he had to admit a couple hours later, one of Aaron's better efforts. The music was loud, the girls weren't bad at all, and Aaron had a pretty sweet setup in the house he was renting in Newmarket. Every randy teenage boy's dream, in fact. Hemi chalked the cue, lined up his shot, and sent another ball into the side pocket, then stood up, grabbed his beer, and took a long pull as he checked out the table.

He heard the shriek and stood, cue in one hand, his beer forgotten halfway to his lips, as the blonde at the air hockey table across from him lunged ineffectually after the caroming puck that crashed into its slot. She threw down her mallet in exaggerated despair, did some pouting, and flounced around a bit, which was all a pretty entertaining sight.

And then it got better, because she heaved a mighty sigh, crossed her arms over her chest and shimmied the tight, low-cut black top up past the black bra with its red lace trim that Hemi had been catching glimpses of all evening, and there was no chance he was going to stop looking now. She tossed it to one side, leaving her clad only in the bra, a little plaid pleated skirt that had clearly been designed with a naughty schoolgirl vibe in mind, and black over-the-knee stockings that were doing the business as well. Hemi had a feeling they'd be seeing whatever was under the skirt pretty soon, because she was fairly well away, and she didn't seem to be trying that hard to win.

"I'm so *terrible*," she wailed, an expression of comical distress twisting her bee-stung lips.

"Nah, darling," Nikau said soothingly from opposite her, not bothering to hide his grin. "Good as gold. You just keep on playing. You're distracting me so well, I'm bound to start losing any time now, have to start getting my own kit off, tragic as the idea is. I hate to lose, all of us boys do. That's the competitive fire in us. When we do, it's a sad, sad experience. Think you can help me out with that, if it happens? Because that's what I'm counting on."

"Well…" A saucy smile curved her pretty mouth, and the wicked gleam in her blue eyes told Hemi that she had plans of her own for this party. She picked up her mallet again. "We'll see. And you shouldn't have told me that. Now I've got a psychological advantage."

"Oh, sweetheart," Nikau said, "you've had that from the start."

She laughed, tossed her head of streaked blonde hair a bit, and cast a coy glance over her shoulder at the pool table, because Hemi and Nikau weren't the only ones looking at her. "Is that right? You'd better look out, then, because I'm coming after you. I'm going to win, and then maybe, if you ask me very nicely, I'll see what I can do about your sad experience."

"You playing pool, mate," Drew Callahan said opposite Hemi, amusement lurking in the gray eyes, "or watching?"

Hemi grinned back at his skipper, appointed only this season and already looking like he'd been born into the job. Not looking a bit pissed, either, whereas the three or four beers Hemi had had, on top of the tough match, were already having their effect. "Call it a break," he suggested.

"Yeh," Drew said. "Break's over. Play pool."

Hemi lost, not that it was a big surprise. Because the girl—Lexi, he thought her name was—*was* bad at air hockey, and before long, the skirt had joined the shirt, and it was just bra, undies, and those over-the-knee black stockings, and, well, he'd just say it was a good look on her.

Nikau had lost his own shirt, but Hemi wouldn't have said he'd been trying as hard as he could have. More being efficient, getting his kit off ahead of time. The music was pumping, his teammates were wandering in and out, accompanied by what Hemi was beginning to suspect was half the off-duty personnel of the local Showgirls franchise and a fair few of their friends, just as Aaron had promised. Plenty of entertainment for just about every unpartnered member of the Blues squad, most of whom were here tonight.

"Another game?" Drew asked. Still annoyingly sober, Hemi realized through the haze of his own beer goggles. Good for a beer and a laugh and not much more, not when anybody was there to watch. Hemi knew that Drew had his own wild side—and a real weakness for blondes, because Hemi hadn't been the only one looking. But whatever Drew got up to, he was always discreet.

"Nah." Hemi set his cue back in the rack with some effort. "I've had a skinful. Going to call it a night. You?" He nodded in Lexi's direction. "Don't want to...party?"

Drew's lips twisted. "Let's say I'm more about exclusivity. Didn't know you were, though."

"Yeh, well." Hemi shrugged. "I'm done for tonight, anyway."

Drew looked at him dubiously. "Need a lift?"

"Nah. I'll just have a bit of a lie-down."

Drew hesitated a moment, and Hemi could almost read his thoughts. "No worries," he told his skipper. "It's all ka pai."

Well, maybe not all. There was a couple on the couch doing some fairly serious snogging, a few more doing some very dirty dancing in the lounge, and Lexi had just missed another shot that had whizzed straight under the toned body she'd flung forward in her attempt to block it, leaving her perched on her tiptoes and sprawled across the table in her heels and very little else, because she'd lost both stockings, and what was coming off next was going to be pretty interesting. In short, things were looking like being out of control at this party in a hurry.

A year ago, Hemi'd have been right in there with the rest of them. Now...well, he was watching, couldn't help that. But that seemed to be all he was doing.

He wandered out into the passage, eventually, finishing off his latest beer along the way, found the stairs, and lifted his feet with care onto each riser. Geez, he was pissed. He opened the door to a bedroom and shut it again pretty smartly. Whoops. Eventually, though, he found an empty room and collapsed on the bed without bothering with the covers.

Somebody ought to turn the music down before the neighbors rang the police, he thought fuzzily, and that was about the last thing he did think. For a while.

Until the girls turned up.

repercussions

♡

"Thanks for coming," Ana said on Sunday afternoon, opening the door to Reka's knock with Tamati over her shoulder, looking back the other way. "Tai! Stop it!"

"Thought Auntie Kiri was taking the kids," Reka said.

"Yeh." It was a sigh. "She had to go over to the Vortex. Somebody didn't come in. Again."

"Training café," Reka said. "Training them to show up, more like. Or trying to." She reached for the baby, jogged him up and down in her arms, saw his little face light up with the beauty of his smile. Oh, how she'd miss her nephews when they left. Her heart twisted at the thought of it.

"Uncle Matiu said he'd take them," Ana went on, "but I'm waiting till Tamati goes down for his nap. He can't handle both."

"Well, then," Reka said, "want me to pack, or mind kids?"

"Pack, please," Ana said. "It's just…so *much*. I weeded down, and weeded down, and I can't see how we still have so much. Most of it's rubbish, I know that, but not rubbish I can afford to buy all over again. And how're we going to fit it all into the flat?"

"Easy as," Reka said bracingly as they moved into the jungle of pasteboard boxes and piles of gear, with Tai bang in the middle of it all. He'd dumped a pile of mini racecars out of a plastic bag, was sending them on a noisy journey around a pile of his baby brother's clothes and up onto a stack of books.

Reka left him to it. He had to do something, and this was less destructive than some games he could be playing. She dropped to her knees and began to sort the haphazard piles into reasonable categories. "You've had most of their things in two rooms of the house," she told her cousin as she did it, "and you're moving into a two-bedroom flat. Same space. It just looks bad because you don't have it shoved into drawers, that's all. Got a marker for these boxes?"

"Um…" Ana looked around vaguely. "Desk, maybe."

Reka didn't waste any more time, just got stuck in. Ana's man Joseph had insisted, on hearing the news about Tai's near escape, that it was time for the family to be together again, and Ana, despite her doubts and fears about leaving her native country, had acquiesced.

"Wish we didn't have to go," she sighed now, sitting cross-legged on the floor and beginning to feed Tamati. "But it's too hard, being alone. Even though I'm not alone, because I'm with Mum and Uncle Matiu, and you, and all the cousins, and there I'll just be with Joseph. Am I doing the right thing, d'you think?"

"Just with Joseph, and the kids, and half the rest of En Zed," Reka reminded her. "Everyone'll be in the same boat, surely. Missing the whanau, helping each other out. They're still Maori, aren't they. You'll be having a hangi before you know it. Roast kangaroo." She grinned at her cousin. "I hear it tastes like chicken."

"Doesn't," Ana said with a reluctant smile. "More like venison, if anything."

"There you go." Reka had found the marker, was filling a box with books and toys. This wouldn't be too bad, not really. A couple hours, and she'd have Ana sorted. It was a good move. Families were meant to be together.

Ana finished feeding the baby, put him down for his nap, and Uncle Matiu came in from his garden and took Tai back to the bedroom, and it went faster with the two of them working, though Ana was still quiet, subdued. Overwhelmed, Reka thought.

"Need to tell you something," Ana said abruptly when they were nearly finished.

"Tell ahead." She hoped Ana wasn't going to confess something Reka didn't need to hear.

"It's about Hemi."

"*Hemi?*" Reka sat back on her heels, her box forgotten.

"You know he had a game last night."

"Yeh. I saw it, at the Duke. Much as I could." Because she'd had a shift, and the bar had been busy. "They won. Preseason, though, doesn't mean much, he said."

"Well…" Ana was fussing unnecessarily with a pile of baby onesies. "You know my cousin Joann, on my dad's side."

"Not so much." Now Reka was confused.

Ana waved a hand. "Yeh. Third cousin, I guess she is. Well, she's got a friend from school days, a bit of a party girl. Joann rang me today from Auckland, told me her friend was meant to meet her for breakfast this morning, and begged off. Said she was out late at a party last night. Quite the piss-up, she said."

"Uh-huh," Reka said. "And this is about Hemi how?"

"It was a party with some of the Blues," Ana said, still not looking her in the eye. "After the match, and Hemi was one of them. Joann was just telling me, you know, the way you do. Chatting. Gossip."

"Oh." Reka forced herself to start her packing again. "Well, I guess they do have some parties."

"I hate to tell you this," Ana said. "Been asking myself over and over what the best thing is. But if it were me, if it were Joseph…And knowing what happened before."

"Just tell me," Reka said, the cold beginning to seep in. "Come on."

"She said, Joann said her mate said, that it was late, and she thought Hemi'd gone. And then she was upstairs, in the toilet, and two girls came out of a bedroom. Half-dressed, she said. Talking about him. About…being with him, in there."

"Two girls," Reka said, her hands still moving mechanically, heedless of the ice that had gripped her heart. "Not even one."

"Yeh. Well, he's a sportsman," Ana said. "Worse, he's an All Black. Could be they all do it. Could be their partners just put up with it, who knows. But I thought you should know. I thought I should tell you. I'll never forget how he saved Tai, and I'll always be grateful to him for that. But…"

"Yeh. Thanks." Reka turned away, pulled another box towards her, and set her chin. "Let's finish this. I have work tomorrow."

"And Hemi coming, don't you?" Ana asked tentatively. "What are you going to say to him?"

"Dunno. But I'm sure I'll think of something."

♡

She'd done it again, she raged at herself as she walked home across the garden, when she permitted herself the luxury of thinking about it, and wished she hadn't. Let herself fall, just like the last time, just like she'd done so many times, and how stupid was she, to keep making the same mistake over and over and over again? Falling for a handsome face and a fit body, mistaking heat for warmth, urgency for connection, and paying the price. Always paying the price, because that was what happened when you led with your heart instead of your head.

She went to work the next morning as usual, put what she'd heard, what she knew, what she'd lost into the back of her mind, because her kids needed her. But by the time she walked home at four, the effort it had taken not to fall apart all day had taken its toll, feet felt leaden, and the thought of seeing Hemi, of telling him what she knew, saying what she knew she had to say, made her heart hurt with a pain so strong, she had all she could do not to clutch at her chest with it. And that made her even angrier. At him, and at herself.

She considered getting made up for him, but what was the point? She changed into a sundress, because it was warm, left her hair in its knot, her feet bare. And when he knocked on the door, she opened it, and the anger and sorrow and trepidation over what was coming just about knocked her down.

The broad smile that met her turned cautious as he read her expression. "Something wrong?" he hazarded. "Something happen? Your family?"

"Something's wrong," she said, stepping back to let him come inside, wishing that he weren't so big, that he weren't so strong, that he didn't look so good to her, that she didn't wish she could fling herself into his arms and have none of this be true. She didn't want to have this conversation, she wanted it to be the way she'd dreamed it would be, and yet she wanted to tell him, to fling the words at him like spears. She wanted to wound him the way he'd wounded her. "But it's not my family," she told him. "You thought I wouldn't know. Do you think because I don't know, it's all right? It's not all right. It's. Not. All. *Right*."

"What's not?" he asked, standing still, barely inside her doorway and looking nothing but confused. "What's not all right? What the hell are you talking about?"

"That you've been telling me all this, about how you feel about me, being so special, all that, then going off and shagging somebody else. Whoever you can find. Whoever's there," she spat, heedless of the tears in her eyes. "Just like before. Just like always. You told me you've changed, and you haven't. How stupid do you think I am? How bloody stupid?"

"Right now," he said, and his face was grim, set, nothing like the cheerful, charming Hemi she'd known, "I think you're pretty stupid. Because you're talking rubbish. I haven't been shagging anybody, and I'd like to know why you think I have."

"Nobody you thought I'd find out about. You didn't know that one of the girls at that party last night was Ana's cousin's friend, did you? You didn't know I'd hear. You thought I would never know, and that made it all right?"

"*Whose* friend? What?"

"My cousin. Ana. Her cousin Joann has a friend, and the friend was there, one of those girls at that party with you. And she told Joann about those girls in that bedroom with you. And what I want to know," Reka said, not able to help the anguish in her voice, "is why? Why tell me you cared? Why make me believe, if you didn't mean it? Why hurt me like this?" She was crying now, and she was raging, and she couldn't help any of it. "Why, Hemi? Why?"

maori rising

♡

Hemi stared at her, struggling for words. *What? How?* "Why?" He finally managed to echo her question. "I could ask you why, too. Why would you think that could even be true? And how am I meant to defend myself against something like that? Some...story?"

"I don't know," she said, the tears gone, the sarcasm all but dripping off her tongue. "Maybe you could start by telling me you didn't do it. Just as, you know. A suggestion."

"All right. I didn't do it. Satisfied?"

Her chin went straight up at that. "No. I'm not. So Joann's friend just made it up, then? She's not like that, not from what Joann says."

He blew out a frustrated breath. "Joann says. Somebody who wasn't there. She told you what her mate said the mate saw, and that sounds reliable to you? I'll tell you this, if she saw me doing anything with those girls, Joann's mate was doing more than drinking, because it didn't happen. All that's coming to you, what? Third-hand? Fourth-hand? And you'd rather believe that than me telling you?"

"So tell me what happened," Reka insisted, and actually made a beckoning motion at him that had the anger rising higher. "Come on. Tell me."

"What happened is that I got pissed." He saw the roll of her eyes, and he didn't know if he wanted to cuddle her or spank her. Both, probably. Both, definitely. "That's right. I did. It happens. Occasionally a person drinks too much, especially after that person's just played a rugby match, especially if that person might be a little lonely. People have been known to do things they regret later. Even you might've had that happen from time to time, if you cast your mind back."

"Like I did with you," she flashed back. "Thank you *very* much. And, what? You telling me you got pissed and did some other girl like you did me? Oh, wait. *Two* girls. Even better. Goodbye." Her hands were on her hips, and then she reached around him for the door and yanked it open.

"No," he said, not moving from the spot where he was planted, because he'd be damned if he was going down without a fight. His hands curled into fists, the anger going straight there, the tension holding him rigid. "I'm telling you I didn't. I'm telling you I drank too much, and because I'm *not* a fool, not anymore, I didn't drive home. I went to have a kip first, and then I woke up because a couple of girls wandered into the bedroom and decided they'd give it a go, and I threw them out, least I think I did, because they left again. A bit stonkered at the time, though, wasn't I. I could recite the flow of the conversation for you, what I said, what they said, what bloody Joann's bloody mate probably said, except I couldn't, because I don't remember it well enough. Because it was just exactly *nothing.*"

"And that's it?" she demanded. "That's what you've got for me?"

"That's it. That's what I've got, and that's all I'll ever have, and I'm sorry you don't like it, but what am I meant to do about it? It's going to happen. I'm going to be someplace, maybe someplace far away, there are going to be girls around, and some of those girls are going to think it'd be nice to take a tour round the park with an All Black, and I'm going to tell them no, for some reason I don't understand myself at this moment." His voice was getting a little louder, and so what? "Why the hell d'you think I'm coming all this way to see you? If I just wanted to have sex, I could have sex, and I could have it without all this agro. Easy as. Thank you very much, twenty dollars for a taxi and see you later. There you are. Sex. I know how to get it if I want it like that, and what I'm wondering right now is, why the hell not?"

He'd flung the words out, and he'd seen her wince at them, and he hated that he'd said it, but what was he supposed to say? It was the truth.

"You think I don't know that, how easy it is for you?" she said, rallying, because there was nobody tougher than Reka. No matter how much his hands fisted, no matter how angry she could see him getting, she wasn't backing down. "I know that. That's the point."

"You think you know. And you're dead wrong. It's pretty obvious that you think I don't know the difference between sex and...love." There. He'd said it. What more could he do? What more could he say?

"No," she said. "I think you do know the difference. I think you know exactly, and you separate them, and you think that makes it all right. Because it's 'just sex,' and it doesn't matter to you, so it shouldn't matter to me. That's what I think."

"Well, no," he said, the Maori in him rising fast. "Actually, you're dead wrong, not that I think you'll believe me, because it's pretty clear you don't. Yeh, I want to have sex with you. And yeh, I want to have sex, period. Course I do. I'm a *man*, and I'm not a monk. But here I am, drove all this way on my one day off, willing to take you for a swim, out to dinner, kiss you and hold your hand, if that's what I get right now, if that's what it takes, and drive straight back home again. I'm willing to do all that, and it still isn't enough. What would be? What would be enough for you? I'll tell you. Nothing. And if nothing's going to be enough, then forget it. Forget this. I don't need this, and I don't need you. Not if you don't want me. I'm not going to beg."

"Fine," she said, her eyes flashing temper. "You don't need me? I don't need you either. Got along fine without you, haven't I. And I'll keep on getting along."

"Fine," he said back. "Fine. I'm going." He flung the front door open and strode down the footpath to his car, forcing himself not to look back, opened the car door with a jerk that just about took it off, slammed it with enough force to shake him, and took off. He didn't squeal the tires. He was damned if he was going to give her the satisfaction.

Driving to the ferry landing, trying not to speed, and failing, because the anger had to go somewhere, and it was going straight into his right foot, pushing the car too fast around the curves until the screech of tires told him he was too close to the edge and he forced his foot up again, eased off.

How could she say that? How could she think it? When he'd done nothing wrong, nothing at all, nothing but say no, and it wasn't like he hadn't been tempted. Because it had been Lexi, Lexi and a girlfriend, and six months ago... Bloody hell, *three* months ago, he'd have been all over that. All over both of them, and thinking what a lucky bugger he was. Didn't she know that? Couldn't she see?

On the car ferry, getting out for the brief journey because there was no way he could sit still. Staring over the rail at the deep green of the bush dotted by the emerald flash of fern trees, the islands of the Bay to either side, all of it receding, because he was leaving it—and Reka—behind.

Those girls. His knuckles shone white on the rail. What would have happened if *he'd* done that? If he and a mate had crawled into bed with a girl who'd been sleeping it off, not in any shape to say no? He'd have been up before a magistrate before you could say Bob's your uncle, that's what, and sent down to play provincial rugby just about that fast, at the very least, his All Black career a thing of the past.

Not that he would have, and why? Because there was a word for that, and he knew what it was. Why was it all right for girls to do it, then? And how could that have been his fault? It was wrong, that was what it was, and if anybody had the right to feel hard done by, it was him.

Back in the car, headed down 12, through Kawakawa and merging onto the motorway towards Auckland, and this wasn't how tonight had been meant to go.

All right, then. Him. He'd known it would be like that. Not like he'd never been to one of Aaron's parties before. He could have done it like Drew, kept himself to a couple beers so he could have left when things started to get out of hand. Drew had never put a foot wrong yet, not in three years in Super Rugby and, yes, three years with the All Blacks as well, selected after exactly one Super match at the ripe old age of twenty-one, and every time since. If he didn't end up as skipper of the ABs this year, Hemi missed his guess, and why? Because he kept his cool head, on the paddock and off it. Because he did it right, because he practiced as hard as he played, because he fronted every single time, every single week, because he was consistent, because he was the definition of steady.

And Hemi was too, he knew he was. He could go all the way, he was dead sure of it. When he laced up his boots, he knew exactly what he was meant to do, what he was going to do, and he went out there and did it, played his game. With flashes of inspiration and improvisation, of course, because that was what a first-five did, but all of it grounded in rock-solid fundamentals, in training and a vision of the game, a knowledge of what was happening around him that you could only have when it was in your bones, when your blood flowed for rugby, when you'd been passing and catching and kicking the ball since you were three, until it felt like an extension of your body when it came into your hands and flicked off your fingertips again, exactly where it was meant to go.

So, yeh. He had that, he knew he did. The bush rolled past him, all the shades of green that were New Zealand, that were Northland, and he realized with a jolt that it was the same thing with Reka. Exactly the same thing. It was the difference between doing it for fun, and doing it for real.

Playing rugby for fun…just about every Kiwi boy did that. But playing it at the level he did was something else. If you didn't have what it took, not just physically but mentally, you'd find out soon enough. If you didn't have the fire, if you didn't have the commitment and the discipline. Body, mind, and soul.

Whangarei had long since receded in the rear-view mirror, Auckland was ever-closer ahead, the day was fading into dusk, and he'd been in the car for half of it, and he was going to be there for longer, because he was exiting the motorway, going through the roundabout, and heading north again.

the flounder returns

♡

She'd done a little crying, but after that she'd put herself into the shower, and then her nightdress, trying for briskness even as the unease grew. Had this just been another dream, based on nothing firmer than the shifting sands of Russell Harbour? Or had Hemi been telling the truth? She didn't know, not anymore, but one thing was sure, he'd left. He was gone.

She got tired of trying to sort it out and went to bed, even though it was only nine-thirty. Nothing to stay awake for, after all. No swimming and touching and kissing with Hemi, because who wanted to be just another notch in his bedpost? Not her, not again. And anyway, he was gone.

She heard the rattle against her window and woke from the doze she'd finally managed to fall into. What? A storm?

What came next wasn't a rattle. It was a *crack,* sharp, loud, and unmistakable. She bolted upright and was out of bed in a heartbeat, and headed for the window.

"*Ow.*" She cut the wail off fast, because Sonya would be asleep downstairs. She limped to the door, turned on the light, and stared at the stone on which she'd banged her toe. And the shards of glass surrounding it.

She skirted the winking splinters carefully, fuming. Tonight, of all night. Kids, larking about, or worse. She grabbed jandals from her closet, shoved them on her feet, then crunched her way to the window and looked out, cautious of the jagged hole in the pane, and belatedly realizing she was wearing only a short, sleeveless white nightdress. Well, bugger it. That might keep their attention while she gave them the earbashing they deserved.

It wasn't kids down there, though. It was Hemi, and the softest hands in New Zealand rugby had just thrown a bloody great stone through her window.

"Sorry," he said, and that was about the lamest thing she'd ever heard. "You all right? Don't cut yourself. There's glass."

"Yeh," she hissed, trying to keep her voice down. "Noticed there was glass, didn't I. Why are you here? What are you *doing?*"

"Reka?" It was Auntie Kiri, pulling her dressing gown closed, coming down the steps onto the drive between the houses, pulling up short at the sight of Hemi. "What's happened? Everything all right?"

"Oh, everything's fine," Reka said. "Some fool just threw a stone through my window, that's all."

"That would be me," Hemi said. "Accident. Sorry."

"What's an accident?" Now Uncle Matiu was there, feeling his way down the steps in the dark, clutching at the banister, and Hemi hurried to help him, and this was nothing but ridiculous.

"Hemi's broken Reka's window," Auntie Kiri said. "Broken her heart, too, hasn't he. That's what he calls romance, I guess. That's his idea of love."

"Oh, is *that* what it is," Reka said.

"Yeh," Hemi said, his upturned face shadowy in the dim light shining out of the open door of Auntie Kiri's house. "It is. And if you'll come down, I'll tell you about it. Please."

"Going to fix her window?" Uncle Matiu demanded.

"Never mind her window," Auntie Kiri said. "What else are you going to do, and not do? You've done wrong, boy, and you'd better be here trying to make it right, and I wouldn't call breaking a window a good start. You saved my grandson, and I never thought I'd say this after the debt I owe you for that, but you've shamed your family with what you've done, and you've shamed Reka."

"What?" Uncle Matiu demanded. "What did he do?"

"Been a dickhead," Auntie Kiri said, and Reka could see Hemi's mouth drop open, the protest beginning. "Been sleeping around, thinking she wouldn't know, just like before."

"Aw, mate," Uncle Matiu said sorrowfully. "That's no good. What would your mum and dad say about that?"

"They wouldn't say anything," Hemi said. "Sir," he added hastily. "Because I didn't do it. I didn't do anything."

"Didn't, eh," Uncle Matiu said, his hooded tortoise eyes blinking slowly at Hemi. "Then why does she think you did?"

"That's what I want to tell her," Hemi said, the frustration clear. "If she'd just come down."

"You did break her window, though," Auntie Kiri said, her tone still suspicious, because she wasn't convinced, Reka could tell.

"What window?"

Reka heard the new voice, tried to see, but she didn't dare get closer to the jagged shards of glass still stuck to the window frame, and her landlady must be standing in the doorway, and she was out of Reka's view. The sharp voice rang out clearly through the quiet Russell night. "Who's broken a window? What's happening?"

"Hemi here," Uncle Matiu said before Hemi could answer, "seems to've thrown a stone through Reka's window."

"Through *my* window, you mean," Sonya said, and she'd come forward far enough that Reka could see her rounding on Hemi. "What d'you mean to do about that, young man? Window glass isn't cheap, and why ever would you do such a thing in the first place? Can't tell me that's accidental. On the first floor? I don't think so."

Her excitable landlady was working herself up into a state, and Hemi had his hands out in front of him, his posture so ridiculously defensive that Reka was having a hard time not laughing.

"Nah," he said. "Not an accident. That is, breaking it was an accident. I was just trying to wake her up, without waking you."

A snort from below. "Pretty good fist you made of that, then, didn't you? Woke the whole neighborhood, and broken glass to boot. Who are you, anyway? Do I know you? Who's your family?"

"Hemi Ranapia," he said. "Not from here. My family's in Ahipara."

"The All Black," Auntie Kiri put in before Hemi could bow to the pressure and begin reciting his entire whakapapa.

"An All Black, and you behave like that?" Sonya asked, her voice rising even further. "That's disgraceful."

"An accident," Hemi said again. He cast a hunted glance upwards. "Reka, come on, baby. Please, come down and talk to me." He was trying a smile. "This is the worst thing I've done, I promise, other than running out on you tonight. Let me tell you. Please."

She couldn't really leave him down there like that, could she? She went to her closet for her dressing gown, pulled it on and went down the stairs, then out through the open door past Sonya, standing at the edge of the porch with her hands on her hips.

"Who's going to pay for my window, that's what I want to know," her landlady demanded.

"I'll pay for the window," Hemi said. "I promise."

Auntie Kiri snorted. "Much good your promises are."

"They are," Hemi said, and Reka walked down the steps and up the driveway to him, because he'd come back, and she needed to hear what he had to say, and, if the truth were known, she had to walk to him. "My promises are good," he said, and he was looking at her now. "Always."

Uncle Matiu looked between the two of them, at Hemi's hand that had come out to hold Reka's, at her fingers that couldn't help curling around his, that couldn't help needing the connection, and gave a single slow nod. "All right, then," he said. "Come on, then, Kiri. Leave these two to it."

"You're just going to leave her out here with him?" Sonya demanded. "When he could be violent?"

"He's not violent," Uncle Matiu said. "Go to bed, Sonya. You too, Kiri. Let Reka handle her man."

"Not my man," Reka muttered, and Hemi squeezed her hand more tightly, and looked down at her, and said, "Yes. I am," and her heart gave a leap in her chest despite everything.

"Goodnight, then," Uncle Matiu said, holding the door for Auntie Kiri and standing there, implacable and unmoving, until she walked reluctantly through it.

He nodded firmly at Sonya, and, with a last dark glare at Hemi, she too retreated into her own house. Then he looked back at Hemi.

"E kore te patiki e hoki ki tona puehu." The Maori rolled sonorously, as always, off his ancient tongue.

"No worries," Hemi said. "I know."

The flounder does not return to his dust. Do not make the same mistake twice. Uncle Matiu had a proverb for every occasion.

He'd told Hemi, but Reka very much feared that he should have told her, because she was the one who needed to hear it.

"Right," she said, walking back to the porch, sinking down onto the second-lowest step and wrapping her dressing gown around her. It was hard to be at your severest when you were wearing a yellow-flowered dressing gown, you had not a lick of makeup on, and your hair was rumpled around your face, but she pulled herself up straight and tall and did her best. "Tell me. Why've you come back? What's changed?"

"Nothing, really," he said slowly, sitting down next to her and taking her hand again, and no matter what, it felt good, warm and strong around her own, and he didn't seem to care a bit about her hair or her makeup. "Guess it's just that I was driving home, and I thought, do I want to be right, or do I want you? And I want you."

That wasn't what she'd expected to hear, and she struggled to find an answer. He waited a moment, then went on.

"I should've stopped, explained better, but I lost my temper. But here's what happened. I drank too much, which I probably shouldn't have done, and I went to sleep, and a couple girls, yeh, came into the bedroom, Joann's mate was right about that. And like I said, I turfed them out again, because I wasn't interested. Or I was, a bit," he confessed. "But it wasn't worth it."

There he was, being honest with her again, and how could she stay angry when he did that, looked at her like that, like he cared so much?

His grip on his hand was urgent as he continued, his gaze steady. "It wasn't worth losing you over, or feeling like I was cheating, or just feeling like I was...doing something I don't want to do anymore. And I wish I could explain it better than that, but I can't. Because I *was* pissed, and I was asleep. And when you didn't even believe me, didn't believe I'd said no, I lost my temper, because it's a big change, and I've made it for you, and you didn't seem to know it, or appreciate it, and I don't know how to make you."

"I appreciate it," she said softly. And I need to say..."
She blinked the tears away, and could almost hear the thudding of her heart. "I need to say that I should've listened. You were here, you're right. You were here, you came all this way. It's just...what Ana said *sounded* true."

"Maybe it would've been true, a few months ago," he said, and her hand jerked a little in his. "But it isn't true anymore," he went on quickly, "and I'd like to know why you thought it was. I would think I might've earned some trust by now. I can see why I hadn't, there at the start, but now? Why not?"

"Because..." she began, then stopped.

"Because what? Why wouldn't you believe me? It didn't make sense."

She sighed, looked down at their joined hands. "Because it happened before."

"Somebody cheated on you."

She swallowed. "Yeh."

"And it was bad." He was rubbing his fingers over her knuckles, and it was so comforting. He'd told her, he'd been honest. Time to harden up and tell him.

"You know that Ana's man is in Perth," she began.

"Yeh. Wait. Your partner cheated on you with your cousin?"

"No." She frowned at him. "Think I'd be that forgiving? Trust me. I'm not that forgiving."

"Course you aren't." His teeth flashed white in the darkness, and then he was scooting a bit closer, turning to face her. "Tell me."

"My partner, Lachlan. A mate of Joseph's. Well, everybody from here who's over there is a mate of Joseph's, aren't they. Not like Russell's a big place." She was rambling. "He was my boyfriend in high school, and then we... reconnected again, after Uni, when I moved back here, and it was good again. Like you. We were apart, and we came back together, and I thought it was all good. And then when he went to Aussie a couple years later for the work, I'd visit him, you know, the way you do, and he'd come back for the family times. I thought we'd get married, one day. I had...dreams. Picked out kids' names, all the things girls do. Stupid. I was so bloody blind, even when he said he had a shift so I couldn't come after all, even when...I was so *stupid.*"

"Not stupid. Normal. And this bloke was a fool, what you're telling me. Didn't know what he had. When?"

"Just before I met you. The first time." She forced herself to look him square in the face. "Why I did what I did. Trying to show myself I was still desirable, to think that a man would still want me. Stupid again. Stupid way to do it, because a man'll shag anything, won't he, anything as available as I was. Doesn't prove a thing."

"Aw, baby," he said, the distress clear. "Don't do that. You were beautiful, and you still are. So beautiful. Any man would want you. Any man would be a fool to let you go. I was, and so was he, if that's what he did."

"Thanks," she said, and if it was shaky, well, so was she. "Anyway. He'd been telling me he was lonely, how bored he was, when he wasn't on a shift, nothing to do." She laughed, a sharp sound in the quiet night. "Yeh, right. So I saved up for a flight at the start of the summer holidays, thought I'd surprise him. Flew all the way to Perth with a chilly bin in the overhead compartment, kina and mussels and whitebait to make fritters, that I'd collected myself that morning, just for him, just to make him what he loved, just to make him *feel* loved."

"He was a lucky man," Hemi said.

"Yeh. Well. Got off the plane, got a bus to his flat, because I knew he had a few days off, wanted to surprise him." Another short, sharp laugh. "And I did. His flatmate opened the door, and I surprised *him,* all right. Told me Lachlan wasn't there, and I said, all right, I'd wait, and he looked so uncomfortable, I knew something was up."

He'd looked more than uncomfortable, she remembered. He'd looked pained, had flapped his hands a bit as she'd come in, sweaty from heaving her burdens up the exterior staircase of the block of flats in the heat of an Aussie summer day, her chilly bin getting heavier with every step, her suitcase bumping along behind her. She'd moved into the lounge with him backing up the entire way before her, coming to a stop next to the grotty green couch, giving her a perfect view of the dirty plates and empty beer cans on the coffee table.

"Really," Chazzer had said, a note of desperation in his voice, shifting from one foot to the other. "I'm about to go out myself."

"No worries," she'd assured him. "I won't nick anything. I'll just stow my things and tidy up a bit."

She'd moved forward, giving him no choice but to step out of the way, had rolled her suitcase and lugged her chilly bin down the narrow passage to the room at the end, had let go of the suitcase to open the door.

And there they'd been. So engrossed, they hadn't even seen her for a few long moments. Lachlan had had his eyes closed, and the girl, whose name she still didn't know, had never wanted to know, had been...busy.

"Let's just say," she told Hemi, "that he wasn't giving her a flute lesson."

"Ouch. That's not good. What did you do?"

She laughed again, and this time, it was real. "Know what I did? Want to know? You sure?"

"Oh, geez," he groaned. "Weaponry. I'll just say again, I didn't do it. I promise."

"No weaponry. Though if I'd had it, who knows? And it wouldn't have been worth it, not for him. Nah. I had my chilly bin, and I used it. You should've seen his face when he got a bin full of kai moana, not to mention all that ice, bang in the nether regions. Screamed like a baby, because kina. Mussels."

"Sharp edges," Hemi said, and he was grinning now. "Spikes. How about her?"

"She was no fool. She'd jumped out of the way. Because I was screaming myself, and he was trying to brush it all off of him, tumbling out of bed, jumping up and down, and if I'd ever loved him, I couldn't have anymore, not after seeing him like that. And then I took my chilly bin and my suitcase and I left him there, and came all the way home again. Cried all the way, raged for a couple days, buried my dreams and went to be a bridesmaid. And did it all again. As you know."

"No," Hemi said. "You didn't. You slept with some-one who saw what you were, everything you are, but who wasn't man enough to appreciate it at the time. I came to my senses, though. I appreciate it now. I'd like to sample your kina and your mussels, and I'll bet you make a hell of a whitebait fritter, too, and I can't wait to try it. But I'll take them *in* my belly, and I'll make sure you want to give them to me that way."

"Maybe I will," she told him, a little smile trying to escape. "Maybe so."

"So that's that," he said. "That's why, and I get it now. And that brings us to our real problem, the one we need to talk about."

"What real problem?" Weren't they done? She just wanted to kiss him, and hold him, and know that she believed him, and know that he knew it too. She wanted to be done fighting. She wanted to make up.

"How are we going to do this, so it works?" he asked. "It's not happening for us, not the way it is, because trust takes…time, and we don't have time."

"We don't?" She was reeling, made to pull her hand from his, but he kept hold of it.

"Nah, wait," he said urgently. "Don't. I don't mean that."

"Then what?"

"I mean, it's not enough time together. You can't see me, where I am, what I'm doing, and I can't see you. You won't sleep with me until you know me, until you trust me. Fair enough, but how are you ever going to know me and trust me if all we ever do is text, a few lines here and there, if we never see each other and don't spend any real time together? How am I going to be able to trust *you?*"

"Me?" It was a punch to the chest. *"Me?"*

"Yeh, you. Why not you? Here I am, gone a couple weeks at a time even during the Super season, and if I'm selected for the ABs again, it's worse. Girls get lonely too. Who says you wouldn't be, and how do I know what you'd do about it? Who says I wouldn't be lying in bed worrying about it in some hotel room in Pretoria or London, nobody to talk to but my ugly roomie, wondering who's chatting you up in the Duke, how good he's looking to you compared to some fella who's never even around? Wondering just how lonely you are by now?"

"You've got some cheek, boy." The anger was back again. "Thinking I'd do that. After what I just said?"

"But I don't know," he tried to explain, "just like you don't. Not really, because we're just getting to know each other, aren't we. We both feel it. It's here, in the puku," he said, touching his belly, "isn't it? For you, like it is for me?"

"Yeh. It is." She was trembling a little now, the chill of the night air, the emotion. She'd been all over the shop tonight.

"We want it, but that isn't enough. So what do we do about that?"

"What *can* we do? Sounds hopeless, if you put it like that."

"Not if you move to Auckland."

"What? Just like that? *Now?*"

"That's what I'm asking. That's what I want." He went on quickly, his voice full of urgency, while she was still trying to digest everything he'd said. "It's three and a half hours each way, and that's too far. I've only got a couple days off a week, if that, and one of them's Monday, and you work on Monday. It doesn't work, don't you see?"

"But…what would I do? Where would I live?"

"Work. And with me."

"Oh, no. With you? Now? Not happening."

"All right. I won't push on that one. But you could live with somebody else. You went to Uni there, surely you know people, could find a flatmate. But you'd see me at the weekend at least, when I'm there, could stay with me then. You could know I'm coming home after the match, and give me something to come home to. You could see, and you could know, and I'd know that you were there too, and bloody hell, Reka, I'd like to know that."

♡

It was a mad plan, and he knew it, and he didn't care.

"Thought you were meant to have a cool head," she tried. "This doesn't sound like a cool head."

"I don't think either of us has a cool head when it comes to the other," he said. "Know I don't. I know I want you. That's what I know. And I know I'm ready to jump in with both feet, see how we go. How about you?"

"We haven't even slept together, except once."

He exhaled sharply. "Again with that? Here I'm meant to be the one obsessed with sex, but it's you who can't get past it. Why d'you think I can't mean this if I'm not sleeping with you yet? Do you think we'll do it, and I'll find out I don't want you? That's not going to happen. I want you, and you want me, and when we do it again, it's going to be so good. And then I'll have you in my bed every night I'm home, and I can't wait."

"Not every night. Like I said."

"Every night I can get you there, and I'll be doing my best to make you want to be there, trust me. And you're stalling. I'm asking you to decide. Right now. Right here. Either we matter, or we don't. Either it's worth the risk, or it isn't." The exultation filled him, the same thrill of commitment he felt when he backed himself, when he *knew* that stabbing the little grubber kick through was the right thing, when he took the risk and went for broke. "I think it's worth it. How about you?"

He saw her still hesitating, still searching his face, and took her hand. "Come on, baby." He softened his tone, tried to send the conviction from his hand to hers. "Come on and give me your heart. I promise to take care of it like it was mine. Better, in fact, because mine, I'm throwing out there. Yours, I'll be holding close. I'll be holding it so carefully. I promise. Let me prove it to you. Come to Auckland so I can. Give us a chance."

fizzing

♡

Five long days later, back at Eden Park in Auckland, and Hemi was bouncing on his toes, waiting to run out of the tunnel, seeing the readiness, the determination in the bodies and faces surrounding him.

Preseason was over, and this was it. Round One, and the boys were fizzing.

Drew gave a quick nod to the group. He didn't speak, because he'd already said everything he had to say. Drew was a follow-me skipper, and it worked. An assistant handed him the ball, and he palmed it in one big hand, led his team out at a trot, and walked to the halfway mark with that assured stride that said he was here, and he was ready, and he'd brought his boys to play, and it was Game On.

It was a fast one, the Hurricanes flashes of yellow. It was obvious from the minute the first lean body leapt into the air, the fullback's sure hands closing around Hemi's opening kickoff, the ball off his boot again in a booming punt, that they meant to play this game at pace. They were a young team, a fast team, and there would be no lengthy back-and-forth exchange of kicks to test the opposition, not tonight.

Hemi was running, shouting to the backs, directing traffic, and it was a ding-dong battle, back and forth. Drew stealing the ball and the Blues on the attack, getting in a few good phases before Kevin McNicholl, the young Blues wing making his first start of his Super 15 career, went down hard in the punishing tackle of Liam Mahaka, and there was a desperate fight for the ball. The second-five got it back to Hemi, barely, and he sent it into touch far downfield, out of the danger zone, and jogged down with the rest of the boys for the lineout.

Fifteen minutes in, the game still scoreless, some hands on hips already on both sides, the forwards blowing hard, and the Hurricanes were past the halfway mark again and coming fast. Nate Torrance, the Hurricanes' second-five, distributed the ball with his usual tidiness, and it was in and out of the hands of a center and off to Aleki Salesa. A hundred twenty kilos of Samoan winger came charging for Hemi, and he was ready, springing off his toes, calculating angles to take the big man down.

Instead, Aleki pivoted, the sudden change of direction catching Aaron, arriving at the angle to help make the tackle, off guard. Aleki put out a palm and shoved off Aaron's chest, a hard fend, and Aaron went straight backward, dumped on his arse and no help at all.

Aleki was still going, clearly intending to tiptoe his way down the touchline, but Drew was too fast for him. The skipper launched himself like a missile, pulled the winger down, and was instantly over him to try to take the ball.

Aleki's hands were too strong, too sure, and he had the ball back to Nate again. The Hurricanes switched tactics, were using their forwards, trying for brute strength to carry the day, crashing their way into a smothering Blues defense that rallied to meet them twenty meters out from the tryline.

Desperate defense now as the forwards bashed the line again and again, and were pulled down again and again, but they had numbers to the right, Hemi saw. He shouted instructions, sprinted to cover even as Aleki got his hands on the ball and was off that way, then, just before he was tackled, sending it behind his back. The ball went from one set of hands to another, and another still, so fast they barely seemed to touch it until, finally, Finn Douglas, the bruising Blues No. 8, managed to take the ball carrier down before he got the pass off. There was a mighty ker-fuffle on the ground, and Hemi couldn't see who'd come up with the ball.

He was aware of Aaron in the background struggling to get out of the hold of Liam Mahaka, who was making a nuisance of himself again. Aaron was clearly desperate to get to the breakdown and join the fight for the ball, and Mako was clearly not intending to allow it. Mako grabbed at Aaron's leg from the ground and hung on, an illegal move if only the ref saw it, a penalty to the Blues that they sorely needed. Aaron kicked out to rid himself of the obstruction, and Mako still didn't let go, and as Hemi watched, Aaron looked down, his face twisting and mouth moving, and sent his boot straight down with force into Mako's jaw.

Even as it happened, Finn was rolling to his feet with the ball and the ref was blowing the whistle for the turn-over, but the line judge was running onto the field at the same time, talking urgently, and everyone stopped and waited.

Mako was rolling a bit on the turf, grabbing his jaw, the trainer on the ground beside him, but the sturdy hooker was on his feet again, taking a squirt of water and rinsing his mouth, clearly determined to play on.

The ref signaled to Drew. He spoke a few words, and Drew listened, looked grim, nodded once, and the ref was calling, "Blue Seven, please," and beckoning.

"You've stepped on the head," the ref told Aaron. "That's unacceptable." He pulled the red card from his pocket, held it high overhead, and the crowd booed its disapproval. Their opinion didn't matter a bit, though, because there was no appeal possible, and Aaron was trotting off the field, anger radiating from his tense body. Much good that did the rest of the squad.

The Blues would play the remaining fifty minutes of the game with fourteen men. Right now, though, the Hurricanes had a penalty kick, and a minute later, they had the first three points of the match.

It was hanging on, after that. Kevin came up from the wing to fill in the gap in the scrum. It should have been a disadvantage but wasn't, because Kevin had played his schoolboy rugby at flanker, and he was a rock. The scrum was solid, and the game was on again, fourteen men or no. The red card, the numerical disadvantage—it should have put the nail in the Blues' coffin, but instead, everybody was lifting a notch, Hemi could feel it.

Still 0 to 3, five minutes left in the half, and the Hurricanes were still playing fast and aggressive. Too aggressive, because they were offside. An opportunity for a penalty kick, and Hemi didn't take it. Instead, he sent the ball sailing into touch, ten meters out from the try-line, because they didn't need three points, they needed seven.

A throw-in to Finn Douglas, the No. 8's powerful frame lifted high in the lineout by two Blues teammates to allow him to take the ball, and the forwards had set up a rolling maul. Finn had his back to the opposing group and was driving backwards, planting his feet and shoving off, one labored step at a time, using every bit of his considerable strength, the rest of the pack around him, pushing him towards the tryline, relentless, while the Hurricanes did their level best to stop the momentum. And Drew at the rear of the maul, pushing too, ball in hand now, watching and waiting, and, as the structure began to break down, distributing it on its way through one, two, three sets of hands, until it was in Hemi's, and he sent it instantly off his left boot, a perfectly weighted little kick that bounced along the ground and into the corner.

Kevin had been watching, was off the moment the ball was, diving as the opposition met him just that critical fraction of a second too late, because Kevvie was on the ball, his arms wrapped around it.

Try!

Hemi was already there, throwing an arm around Kevin and scrubbing a hand over his sweat-dampened hair while his teammates piled on and the crowd roared. He allowed himself the moment's celebration, then disengaged and walked upfield with the ball, judging the best distance for the tricky angle. That try had been at the screaming edge, barely on the right side of the post, but then, that was why it had been possible.

He took out his mouthguard with deliberate movements, tucked it into the top of his sock, the ritual, as always, calming his mind. He set the tee precisely, positioned the ball on it, then stood well back behind the touchline, looked at the ball, at the posts, breathed in, breathed out, letting the adrenaline settle, allowing his galloping heart to calm. Tuned out the roaring crowd, the Hurricanes in their eager line poised to rush him and charge down the kick, and focused only on the spot where the ball would go.

Three running steps, a swing of his right leg, and the conversion was cleanly between the posts as the hooter sounded to end the first half, and he was tossing the tee aside and trotting off the field. He'd known the moment the kick left his boot, as he always did, hadn't even had to look.

Fourteen men to fifteen, and they had the lead at the half, and they had the momentum. Everything seemed possible tonight. It was all good.

♡

It would have stayed all good, too, if the Hurricanes had been willing to accept their fate, but you didn't make it to Super Rugby by being willing to give up. Instead, the lead changed, back and forth and back again, all through the second half, and more than one set of hands were on top of a player's head during every pause in the play, tortured lungs working, chests heaving to draw in the breath to continue. The strain of covering for a missing forward was beginning to tell on the Blues, and they were down again by two hard-fought points as the scoreboard ticked ever onward until there were bare seconds to play, and this was it. Do or die, and they were nowhere close to the tryline.

Crunch time. Go for the try, or something else? Hemi made his decision, called across to the backs standing nearby, got nods of understanding, and began to plan.

The second-five dug the ball out of the frantic mess of the breakdown, the Hurricanes going for the steal with everything they had, and passed it outside to Kevin. Kevin had it for only a moment, shifted to avoid the onrushing tackler, then sent it back inside to Hemi, a high, looping shot with his right hand over his head like a basketball pass, straight over the two Blues players between and catching the Hurricanes on the hop. They hadn't been expecting this. They'd been thinking of the try, and that made this Hemi's best chance.

He'd practiced it again and again, of course he had, but not with the crowd, not with the noise, not in this moment. He was nearly forty meters out, too far to the left of the posts, and the Hurricanes were coming, but it didn't matter, because the hooter had sounded, and they *were* forty meters out.

He dropped the ball to the ground, sent it off his right boot on the bounce, and not a moment too soon, because all two meters-plus of Andy Cuthbert loomed in front of him, the mighty lock stretching with every last straining bit of his enormous wingspan, leaping to block the drop-goal that would win the game.

The ball cleared Andy's grasping fingers by centi-meters, and Hemi watched its progress as he ran, but he already knew the answer, had known it the moment the ball had left his boot with just that tiny bit too much spin. The crowd was roaring its approval. They didn't know what he knew, but there was still a hope, if he was right.

He saw the ball hit the left post as he'd known it would, and he was there, charging his way to it as it sailed off at a crazy angle, and he was stretching desperately, reaching, leaping.

Not fast enough, not high enough, not far enough. Just that micro-second not fast enough to get it, because the Hurricanes' fullback had been watching too, had seen the angle, had already been in position and been able to leap at the same time and come down with it instead. A kick into touch of his own, and the whistle blew, and the game was over.

Hemi stopped running, stopped trying, put his hands on his hips and blew out the strain of effort, the exhaustion of defeat, because the Blues had lost the first match of the season.

aftermath

♡

Hemi walked the yellow gauntlet of Hurricanes players, shaking hands and exchanging a word and a back slap, the fatigue and pain setting in now that it was all over, but still coming a poor second to the sting of the loss, the disappointment at his own failure.

He willed himself not to feel until he was in the tunnel, heading into the sheds. Once he was stripping down, though, there was no escape, and he wasn't alone, he could tell. It was always a sober group after a loss. They unwound tape and headed to the showers without the laughter and horseplay that would have accompanied a victory, then pulled on their warmups in anticipation of the visit to the Hurricanes, the ritual beer they would share before everyone headed home to lick his wounds.

The rivalry would be left on the field, except for some things. That head-stomp would be remembered, because you didn't do that. They all knew how vulnerable they were out there. Stomping an opponent's face with your sprigs…it was beyond the pale, and everyone knew it.

Drew came over from his locker to sit on the bench beside him, and Hemi tugged his shirt down, looked at him in surprise. "Got the interviews to do, haven't you?" he asked his skipper.

"Yeh," Drew said. "Just stopped to say that it was worth trying. Glad we did it. Give the Sharks something to think about for next week, tell you that."

Hemi nodded. Not much more to say about it. They'd tried, and it hadn't come off. He'd be practicing those drop-goals every day from here on out, and next time, he wouldn't miss.

"Kevvie did well, didn't he?" Drew asked.

"Yeh." They both looked across to a corner of the room, where the young winger sat on the bench, quietly getting his kit on. Not a lick of arrogance to Kevin. Sitting at the front of the bus where he belonged, not inserting himself, listening and soaking it all up. No flash at all, except where it counted.

"Ring you tomorrow," Drew said. "Find out what you're seeing."

Hemi nodded again. He had the feeling they'd both been seeing the same things. Nothing like a stomp to the head and a red card to shine the spotlight. Aaron was headed for the bench at the very least, if not all the way down to provincial rugby. Some players could handle the pressure and pace at Super level, and some couldn't. Aaron, it was becoming clear, couldn't.

On the other hand, despite everything that had happened, and despite the loss, there'd been something out there tonight, something new. A spirit, a tightening of the bond the team shared. It had started with the rock-steadiness from Drew, but everyone else had seen the challenge and had lifted to meet it, and they would remember it. A set-piece that solid, a fight that hard, all the way to the end against an opponent of the Hurricanes' caliber, fourteen men on fifteen—that memory was one they'd draw on in the weeks and months to come. Sometimes a loss got you as far as a win, and this was one of those times.

And Kevin. The kid had been a revelation, as full of running at the end of the night as when he'd started. He had the engine, and he had the same cool head Drew and Hemi shared, the quality you could only coach so far.

A blue head, they called it. The ability to think under the pump, to make logical decisions, to see the entire game. So easy to be a red head instead, to let emotion take over, to let the adrenaline flood and drown out reason, to allow tunnel vision to set in, decision-making to deteriorate. Kevin, despite his ginger hair, despite his youth, was a blue head, and they needed more blue heads on this team.

Drew put a hand on Hemi's shoulder, pushed off to meet the next obligation, the weariness and the professionalism both apparent in the gesture. "See you."

"Yeh," Hemi said, glad it was Drew and not himself facing the cameras, making sense of the night for the journalists—and the public. He pulled out his phone, sent a quick text to Reka.

Not quite what I had in mind. Thanks for coming anyway. See you at breakfast.

He waited a moment, staring at the screen, but didn't get an answer, and shoved the phone back into his pocket. If a man were trying to impress a woman, Hemi's night probably wouldn't have been exactly the way he'd have chosen to do it.

At least she was here. He hadn't got a commitment out of her that night, not what he'd wanted, but he'd got her to come to the game tonight, to stay over the weekend. She was sleeping at a friend's, which was a pity, but he wasn't pushing it, because he wasn't stupid. He was picking her up tomorrow, taking her to breakfast at the Takapuna Beach Café and then showing her his house, and he very much hoped that she'd want the full tour.

He'd spent a couple hours cleaning yesterday, laughing at himself as he hoovered and scrubbed the toilet, thinking how his mum would laugh to see him. But he wanted Reka to think it was…nice. Someplace she could stay. Someplace she could live.

It was Takapuna, at least there was that, and she'd sounded enthusiastic about that bit. She was like him. She needed the sea.

He wasn't going home for a while yet, though, because Aaron didn't limit himself to the single beer after the match that Hemi allowed himself, and Hemi ended up giving him a lift home to Mission Bay, well out of his way. But a postgame summons for drink-driving would be all the team needed to put a final stamp on the night, so despite his disgust, he did it all the same.

It was after eleven-thirty by the time he was across the Harbour Bridge, waiting at the light, indicating for the turn onto the quiet street off Lake Road that ended at the beach. He had to wait for a couple cars to turn ahead of him, unusual for this time of night, but there'd been more traffic than usual. Saturday night at the bars, and a rugby match at Eden Park, a fair few people out on the razzle even in Takapuna.

Finally, he was following the receding taillights down the street, almost home and able to relax, anticipating his bed. Until his eyes, still alert even after the long night, saw the difference in the shadows on his unlit front porch. Surely that was a bulky shape there, nearly hidden under the eaves, where no shape had any right to be.

What the hell?

It was the last straw, and he let the cold rage, denied all night, flood his body. He drove on nearly a block past the house, noting that the car ahead had pulled over too, and the street was empty again.

His heart leapt at a sudden thought, and he pulled his phone out, checked it. No text from Reka. Of course not. It was nearly midnight, and she didn't have a car. It was a nice idea, but it wasn't Reka, and he knew it.

His fingers hesitated a moment, then they were moving, and he'd texted,

R U there?

He waited in the dark, hopeful despite himself, for a long couple of minutes, then shoved the phone back in his pocket. She was in bed, and he had some wanker on his porch. Or somebody dangerous. Even better.

He turned off the dome light so it wouldn't shine and betray his position, then grabbed his bag and got out of the car, shutting the door carefully to avoid the *thunk* that would give him away in the quiet night.

Barely aware of the stiffness that had set in over his forty-minute journey, he crossed the street as far from the glow of the streetlight as he could manage and crept up the footpath, keeping to the shadows of the huge trees that grew in the verge between sidewalk and street, pressing himself close to the walls of concrete and stone that fronted the high-set villas.

He heard something behind him and froze. Footsteps, and he pressed himself against the wall, because who would be walking up the street at midnight? He waited, breath held.

Somebody on his porch, and somebody else behind him. What *was* this? He heard the thudding of his heart, the cicadas, musically shrill in the night, the distant hum of traffic back on Lake. And the footsteps.

He looked back and saw him. One of his neighbors. An older fella, walking a labradoodle. He nearly laughed. He was losing it.

The fella froze himself for a moment at the sight of him, and Hemi realized what he must look like, a big joker like him lurking in the shadows in the middle of the night. He stepped out, keeping his posture casual, turned away from the man, towards his house, and nodded a greeting over his shoulder.

"Evening," he said, and walked on. The footsteps hesitated a moment, then started up again.

Another thirty meters, and Hemi had reached the boundary between his house and his neighbors'. He didn't pause, just walked straight up the footpath to the side gate, tossed his bag across, then got his hands on the top of the wooden obstruction, shoved himself up and swung over, landing on the bricks in a crouch that jarred his sore body.

He left his bag where it had fallen and walked quietly along the brick path that led around the house to the ranch sliders opening onto the back patio. He unlocked the door, slid it open as quietly as he could, stepped inside and slid it shut behind him, flicking the lock with his thumb.

He stood in the silent darkness of the kitchen for a moment, thinking. He could go to bed, leave the visitor out there to rot. He could ring the police, let them deal with it. Neither option was appealing. What he wanted to do was whack into somebody. Failing that, to scare the shit out of him. Never mind that it could be dangerous, that he didn't know what kind of a nutter was lurking out there. He didn't care.

He skirted the kitchen island by feel, walked through the doorway and along the passage to the front door, setting each foot down with stealthy care, pressed his ear to the wood and listened. Nothing.

Slowly, deliberately, enjoying the thought of what was to come, he eased the deadbolt to the left, listened again. Still nothing.

The next moment, he had flung the door wide, jumped out onto the porch, and rushed the figure standing looking out over the street. He got him by the arms and gave him a hard shove, shouting, "Get the fuck out of here!"

Reka. He realized it even as he grabbed her, even as he shoved her, and he was lunging, reaching, falling along with her, because he'd pushed her straight off the porch. They were falling down the broad wooden staircase together, and he was wrapping his arms around her, desperately twisting himself in midair to take the impact.

He hit hard, hip and shoulder, she uttered a sharp cry as she banged down with him, and they were sliding, *thump thump thump,* his legs and back slamming painfully against each riser in turn.

They were at the bottom, rolling a bit, and then she was wrenching herself away, her breath coming in sobbing pants.

"Are you all right?" He reached desperately for her. She had to be all right. She had to. "Baby, I'm sorry. I'm so sorry. "

"Bad...bad time?" she got out.

He laughed out of pure shock. Only Reka. "Nah." He sat, pulling her up with him, the pain forgotten. "Nah. Perfect time."

"Got...some way of...showing it, haven't you?"

He could feel her shaking despite her words. He ran his hands down her arms, trying to check, but it was too dark to really tell. "You hurt?" he insisted. "How bad?"

"Shaken," she said, sounding better. "What about you?"

"A few bumps to add to the tally. No worries. Sore tomorrow anyway."

"This how you always greet visitors?" She was feeling behind her now, patting at her hair. She really was all right, then, and the relief made him sag for a moment.

"Thought you were a stalker," he tried to explain, "or a photographer, maybe, staking out my house. I've had that kind of thing before, and I haven't had...the best night. I texted to see if maybe it was you, no answer."

"Oh." She reached into her pocket and pulled it out. "Out of juice. Huh. I forgot."

He wasn't listening, because she'd been wearing a long, belted coat, her hair in its knot, which was why he hadn't recognized her in the shadows. Now, her hair was falling down a bit, and the coat...

His hand slid inside, where the thing had loosened, because it hadn't been buttoned, closed over the warm, firm skin at her waist, his favorite spot. Well, one of his favorites.

"Baby," he managed. "You've come out without your clothes on."

Her voice had a hitch in it, a little gasp, and it thrilled him, just like always. "That's because...I meant to surprise you. And I did."

"Mmm." He had his other hand at the formerly-tidy knot at the back of her head, was pulling pins out and dropping them, heedless, to the pavement, tugging at her hair so it spilled down her back. His hand was in her hair, then, and he had her face lifted to his, was sitting on the pavement with her half in his lap, eating her up.

She was making some little noises into his mouth, surprise and eagerness and wanting, because Reka couldn't hold back a thing, because she gave up everything, and everything was what he wanted. His hand was moving, there inside her coat, sliding up her side, reveling in the smoothness of her. Tracing over the curve of a breast, feeling her suck in a breath against his mouth as his hand slid inside the bra that was all she had on under her coat, that and a pair of undies, the white lace catching the moonlight, glowing against her dark skin.

Her hands clutched at his shoulders as his own hand continued to stroke, as his thumb flicked a hardened point, because she was so sensitive, so responsive. He remembered that, and he wanted so badly to be reminded some more. His tongue was in her mouth, and hers was playing too, his hand was wrapped in her hair, and in another moment, she was going to be on her back.

"All right there?"

He heard the voice behind him. It wasn't the first time it had spoken, either, but then, he'd been a bit preoccupied.

He turned halfway, not letting go of Reka, keeping her behind him, and it was the fella with the dog. The labradoodle was wagging its curly tail, coming forward on its leash, sticking a curious black nose out to sniff at Hemi.

"I heard some noise," the man said. "Some shouting. Saw somebody jump the fence earlier. All right?" he repeated. "Miss?" he added, trying to get a look at Reka.

He thought Hemi was attacking her, Hemi realized with a cross between astonishment and amusement.

"Yeh." Reka cleared her throat, grabbed the edges of her coat, shifted herself off Hemi, on her knees now and into the man's view. "All good. Just...a little accident. But all good now," she repeated.

"Ah. Well." His neighbor looked between the two of them, and Hemi gave the labradoodle a pat, since it seemed to think that a person on the ground was a person who wanted to play. "This is a quiet neighborhood," the man went on. "You may want to go inside now."

"Ah. Yeh. Good idea." Hemi got to his feet, took Reka by the hand and pulled her up to join him. Her coat wasn't quite closed, and she snatched her hand from his and pulled the edges together, and Hemi stepped in front of her again. "Just going," he told the other man. "Goodnight."

His neighbor nodded and walked on, and Hemi turned and looked at Reka. She was leaning against the pillar at the bottom of the steps, beginning to shake with nearly-silent laughter. It caught him unawares, and he found himself laughing too, because she was infectious, and that spurred her on, until they were both lost.

He looked at her, leaning and laughing and gasping, hugging herself, her hair streaming around her, the lacy bra flashing white in the shadow of that coat, and he forgot to be quiet, the bubble of it rising, swelling, all the way from his belly until he was gasping, leaning against the pillar and laughing just as hard as she was, and a whole lot louder.

"Shh," she said, and giggled, and that was funny too, and made him laugh a little more. "You bad neighbor."

"Can't help it." He pulled her towards him, and she came to him willingly, eagerly, wrapped her arms around his neck and smiled up at him, and he smiled back. "If naked girls are going to turn up at my house in the middle of the night, these things are going to happen."

"Maybe they could start happening now," she said. "Keep a girl waiting, don't you?"

"Nah," he said, still smiling. "Nah."

He was up the stairs with her just like that, pulling her through the door. No more waiting. Time to go.

e ipo

He kicked off his shoes even as he was giving the door a single hard shove, and then he had her against it and was kissing her again. His mouth was on hers, invading, demanding, and she was doing nothing but welcoming him inside.

He stayed there as long as he could stand it, then kissed his way across her cheek to the spot under her ear that she loved. He remembered how she'd moaned the first time he kissed her there, and he was right, because she moaned again now. She sagged a little against the door, her pulse was racing under his mouth, and his own heart was hammering just that hard.

And then his hands had fisted on the lapels of the coat, pulled it wide. He'd have looked at her, but he couldn't look at her and kiss her at the same time, and he couldn't deny himself the pleasure of using his teeth gently on her neck, feeling her head turn, her hands pulling him closer, clutching at his shoulders, trying to get more.

She was pressed against the wood of the door, making some noise now as his hand roamed inside the lace edging of her bra, the other hand coming around from behind to cup her luscious backside, trace over the lace border that didn't reach all the way to her thigh, because those undies were cut high, leaving all that gorgeous bare skin for his hand to explore. Lace bordering silk in both directions, fabric and smooth warm flesh. All she was managing to do was hang on, and he loved it.

He pulled her away from the door, shoved the coat down her arms to fall in a heap on the floor, and then he did look.

She was worth looking at. The bra didn't really do a good enough job of covering her, because there was a bit of brown visible against one white edge, and he was on fire. The undies dipped so close too, there in the center, tracing a path, and he had to take that path. Right now.

He reached around her back, flicked the clasp and undid the bra, pulled it over her arms, and tossed it on top of the coat.

"Aw, sweetheart," he breathed. "That's my girl." He had the perfect round weight of a breast in each hand, and he had to pause a while there, caressing, teasing, playing with her, because his memory hadn't steered him wrong there either. She was exactly that responsive, exactly that deliciously sensitive. Her eyes were closed, her head was back against the door, she was breathing hard already, and they'd barely started.

"I'm going to make you feel so good," he told her, and if it came out a little ragged, who could blame him? "I'm going to do it all to you tonight. We're going to do it until you can't take any more, and then you're going to take it anyway."

"Hemi," she moaned, and he'd never heard anything better. He was going to have to come back to this later, because her back was arching, her lips had parted, and he needed his mouth there as much as she needed him to be there. But he needed something else even more, and he couldn't wait another minute. He ramped up the pressure a little, was getting that little bit rougher that he knew she needed, was pinching a nipple, taking it right up to that knife-edge, that exquisite point just before pleasure became pain, and she was definitely moaning now.

He sent the other hand down, stroking over the velvet skin of her side, the little swell of her belly, and there she was. There was the heart of her, where he had to be.

"So wet," he said, his voice raw in his ears. "So good." He was yanking, and the undies were coming off, down her legs, and she kicked out of them. She was naked, and he still had all his clothes on, because she hadn't been able to do anything more than hang on.

She wasn't going to be able to do anything anytime soon, either. He was dropping to his knees, because he had to have this now. Right now.

"Hemi," she said again, protest or invitation, he couldn't tell, but he had a hand on either thigh, was parting her legs, and she shifted in her heels, still pressed against the door, and let him do it.

He kept a hand on a thigh, held her there while the other began a slow, stealthy journey, exploring, parting, finding his way, in no hurry at all, feeling the way she began to urge him closer with her body, trying to get him where she needed him, making little protesting sounds at his refusal to touch her where she wanted him most. By the time he'd finished teasing her, she was gasping, and when he finally set his mouth to her, she cried out loud.

It didn't take long after that, and that was a pity, because he loved it. She was trembling, jerking against him from the start, going up fast. She started out moaning, and when he sped up, she was calling out, and if his hands hadn't been holding her there, her legs wouldn't have been able to support her, because he could feel them shaking.

And when he got his fingers inside her and began to thrust, she screamed. And she shattered, with so much force, he could hardly hold her. Both her hands fisted in his hair, and she was wailing, shuddering, her back slamming into the door, over and over and over.

He kept on until her shudders had become trembles, until her cries had become little moans again, until he could feel her legs shaking so hard he knew she was about to fall. He pulled her down with him, then. Gently, because she wasn't falling again tonight.

"Hemi," she sighed, lying back against his supporting arm, opening her lustrous brown eyes, trying to smile, but her mouth was still trembling. "I can't...I can't..."

"Yeh," he told her. "You can. You just need me inside you. Then you can."

"Please," she said, and she was begging, and he needed to hear her beg.

"Condom," he realized. "Come on. Bedroom." He pulled her up with him, waited for her to kick off her shoes, took her by the hand, and led the way through the darkened house, up the stairs to the bedroom. So carefully cleaned, the bed neatly made, the bed he'd hoped he'd have her in tomorrow.

Neat no longer. He switched a light on at the bedside with his right hand, his left still clutching hers, yanked the bedclothes back, and pulled her down with him.

Reka, dark against the white sheets, naked and abandoned to her pleasure, all that shining dark hair streaming behind her, around her, wanting him as much as he wanted her. Almost as much, because surely it wasn't possible to want anyone, to crave anyone, to need to be inside anyone as much as he needed to be inside her.

He reached into the bedside table, scrabbled for the packet with fingers that weren't entirely steady, tossed it onto the bed next to her, but she was up now, pulling his jacket off, then on her knees, yanking his shirt up over his head, her hands following it, stroking him, caressing him, so eager to touch him.

She was bending now to kiss his shoulder, her hands still exploring, awakening sensation everywhere they touched, and however much she had needed his hands and mouth on her, he needed hers more.

She seemed to know it, because she was stroking down over his sides, his belly while her mouth followed, and he was the one on his back. She was over him, pulling off his warmup pants, his briefs, and his clothes were on the floor.

She was on top of him, avid, eager, her mouth tracing the whorls of his moko, licking over a nipple and pulling it into her mouth, her tongue working, and he knew why it had felt so good to her, because his hands were the ones tangled in her hair now, and all his attention was there. Right there. There, and on the hand that was sliding down his chest, his ribs, his abdomen, lower and lower, until all he could think of was that mouth, and that hand, and where that hand was going.

She paused, stroked his hip with long, sensitive fingers. On down to the muscles of his outer thigh, then up, sliding over the quadriceps. Down again, then tracing delicately over his inner thigh, and her mouth, her tongue were working on him.

He was the one who was helpless now. "Reka," he gasped, shifting on the bed, trying to get closer to that hand.

"Say please," she murmured against him. Still too far away. Too far, and he needed her. He *needed* her.

"Ah. Please," he said, because he'd have said anything, and he felt her smile against him, and then her hand was there, where he needed her, and he rose into it, and she began to stroke, started to kiss her way down his chest, down his belly, her mouth following the path her hand had blazed.

"Do you want this?" she asked when she was there, her mouth already against him, so close and still not quite there, her voice like cream. "Do you want to come in my mouth?"

The jolt of it ran all the way through his body. "Yes," he got out. "Yes. Yes."

"Then come on, boy," she said. "Give it to me."

She set in on him, worked him over, and he was lost, and he did.

And this time, he was the one shouting.

♡

Because I'm a good time, she'd told him, what felt like months ago. *Because I'll do anything.* And it was true.

They'd taken a shower, later, but then they'd been clean, and soapy and slippery, and it had seemed like a shame to waste that. He'd had her against the wall again, the water beating down, her legs wrapped around his waist, the power of it taking her over until she'd been wracked with it, and if he hadn't held onto her afterwards, she'd have been taking her second tumble of the night, because all her strength was gone, drained, pulled out of her body by pleasure.

He helped her out of the big stone stall, dried her off with a big, fluffy towel that she'd have sworn was brand-new, led her to the bed again and climbed in with her, pulling the duvet over them and settling down beside her, holding her so close, running a hand over her skin, and she was all but purring with relaxed contentment.

"You make me feel so good," he told her after a minute. "and you make me so...you make me lose it. I want so much."

"Mmm." She cuddled a little closer. "You can have it, too. Seems you can do anything you want with me. I'm just that easy after all, when it comes to you."

"I am a lucky man," he said with a sigh, and she looked up at him, saw the look of smug satisfaction on his face, and laughed a little.

"Just you remember that," she told him as severely as she could manage.

"You'll remind me if I forget, I'm sure. And we forgot the condom that time," he added lazily, his hand smoothing her hair now, "in the shower."

"We? That wasn't me, boy."

He laughed, a low chuckle. "Yeh. Me. I forgot."

"You don't sound too worried," she decided.

"I'm not. I'm clean, and as I may have mentioned, I've been waiting for you."

"That's not the only thing condoms are for."

"Not worried about that either."

"Well, as it happens," she admitted, "you don't need to be, because I'm all good on that. But good to know, because I come from a fertile family. I should warn you."

"Told you. I'm not worried." His hand stroked over her shoulder, like he still needed to touch her. "I'm happy, is what I am. But why tonight? What changed your mind?"

She lay still for a moment. "I wanted to be here," she said slowly, serious now. "I wanted to be here for you. I figured, you probably had people there for you when you won, happy to celebrate with you. I wanted you to know you had somebody there when you lost. *I* wanted to be there for you."

"Aw, baby," he said, and then he was laughing a little again.

"What?" she demanded, although she was smiling back. "Making my declaration, aren't I?"

"If I'd known all I had to do was lose," he said, "this would have been a whole lot easier."

She was lying there a bit later still, somewhere in the depths of the night. They'd slept, and woken up, and he'd reached for her, and it had all happened again, so sweet this time, touches and murmurs and a slow, strong rock into the blissful ache of release. Now, she was sprawled over him and loving being there, the beat of his heart steady and strong under her ear, already slowing even as her own heart continued to pound.

She traced a hand lazily over his heavy shoulder, down the sculpted muscle of his arm, reveling in the solidity of his warm body beneath her, in the certainty that he was hers, and that he wanted to be.

"Whoa, boy," she said on a sigh, "you take my breath away."

A quick jerk of his chest under her cheek as he laughed. "Aw, sweetheart. You have no idea what you do to me."

"Mmm." She smiled against his skin, gave him one last gentle kiss there. Both of them finally sated, bodies humming with satisfaction. And falling asleep with him holding her…it was everything she'd ever wanted.

His hand moved down her back, caressed its way down to her waist, settled there as if that were his place, and that was how it felt. Like his.

He spoke, so quietly she could barely hear him.

"E ipo," he said, and then, more softly still, "Kia hei taku ate i te tau o tana tiki."

She raised her head from his chest to look at him, her hand still stroking the intricate designs of the tattoo that swirled over his beating heart, needing to touch him there, and his hand smoothed her hair as if he needed the same thing.

My darling, he'd said. *Let my heart be bound with the strings of her tiki.*

It was from a poem, a poem she'd never have dreamt Hemi knew, one that she would never have imagined him saying to her.

"Time to tell me too," he said, and she looked at him and could see straight through the outward assurance to the trembling heart beneath, the heart that needed hers as desperately as she craved his own.

She gave it to him, because it wasn't a choice.

"Ka nui taku aroha ki a koe," she told him, the tenderness so strong, the longing to hold his vulnerable heart, to protect it forever, so fierce.

She saw his eyes close for a moment, and she could tell, all the way to her belly, all the way to the seat of her soul, that she was watching the fear of love unreturned leaving him, flying away on eager wings. The relief flooding his body was as real to her as if it were her own, because it was.

My love for you is limitless, she had told him.

Because it was.

epilogue

♡

October. Spring, and the first real break of the season for an international player, the gap between the end of the Southern Hemisphere Rugby Championship and the beginning of the five-week European Tour allowing for a much-needed rest, precious time with family and friends away from the pressure of the game.

A break, and he needed a break, for all sorts of reasons. Two weeks off, and he was spending them with Reka.

They'd gone to Whangarei first to visit her mum, to Russell to see the rest of her whanau, and she'd cried a little when they'd left both places.

"It's only a few hours away," he said when they were in the car again, across on the ferry, on their way north to Ahipara and his own family. "You can still visit heaps. It's all good, baby."

"Not what you said when you told me to move." She was drying her eyes already, throwing it right back at him. Bloody hell, but he'd missed this.

He laughed. "Got me. And I didn't tell you to move, I asked you. I only wish it were that simple." Even though he didn't, not really. "But yeh, living with the people you love is better. Which is why I want you to live with me."

"Oh, smooth," she said. "Dead smooth. Got me there, didn't you, in the end. Got my toothbrush in your bathroom."

"And your nightie in my closet, and I'm happy to have it there. I'll be happier when all your things are there, though. I'll be happier when you're there even when I'm not."

"I know you would, and you're wearing me down, no worries."

"Good." He took a hand off the wheel to squeeze hers for a moment, then had to put it back again, because the road had too many twists and turns in it for one-handed driving, this far north.

Slowing for the drive through the minimal bustle that was Kaitaia, around another green curve, and, finally, it was there, the exhilarating tang that was salt and ozone and endless possibility, filling his lungs even before it came into view, and his heart lifted as it always did at the sight and the smell and the sound of the sea.

His sea. His beach. His place. The sweep of gold meeting blue that stretched endlessly northward, uninterrupted, all the way to Cape Reinga. The Ninety-Mile Beach.

"Home," Reka said, as always understanding him perfectly.

"Yeh," he said. "Home."

♡

After that, it was his mum running out to greet them, arms wide and welcoming, telling them about the hangi she had planned for the next day. Going out fishing with his dad, helping him rebuild the carburetor on a faulty outboard motor, eating and talking and laughing and his whanau, the neighbors, the friends, the land and the sea.

Home, and Reka fit there, the same way he fit with her family, understanding and belonging and meshing at a level, in a place that was bone-deep. Spirit-deep. Blood-deep.

♡

"Hope you aren't planning to get us stuck," she told him a few days later as they drove along the beach. How many days, he'd have had to stop and count, because one day blended into the next here, slipped by so easily.

"Do me a favor," he said with exaggerated pain, steering expertly around a soft spot, heading briefly towards the water and then back higher up the sand again. "I grew up driving this beach. Can't tell you how many tourists I've dug out in my time. That's why there's a shovel in the boot. For them, not us."

"You just tell yourself that." She was laughing, and the sound, as always, made him smile too. "Luckily, I'm a dab hand with a spade."

"You're asking for it," he warned, doing his best to sound menacing.

"Oh, yeh, big boy. I'm so scared. Who knows, you may push me down the stairs again."

"I thought we'd agreed to forget that," he complained. "You're going to be bringing that up for years, aren't you?"

"Probably." Her smile was a bit smug now. "Nah. Definitely."

"Just you remember," he warned her, "I'm good at discipline. For myself, and for...others."

"And again," she said, "not exactly quaking in my boots. Going to have to do better than that."

He had to laugh. "I'll think of something, then, shall I?"

"You do that," she said. "Something to impress me. Thrill me a little, too. Later."

They stopped along the way to toboggan down the sand dunes of Te Paki, and Reka loved it as much as he'd known she would, charged up the steep slope without any trouble at all, again and again, making easy work of the heavy going through the deep sand. And slid down every bit as fast as he did, laughing with the exhilaration of speed, hitting a bump once, accidentally or on purpose he couldn't tell, rising in the air, coming down to one side of her sled and rolling, over and over, down to the bottom of the huge hill.

She got up laughing, too, grabbed her toboggan and jumped out of the path of a shrieking pair of young girls, and ran down the slope to join him at the bottom, her hair and clothes a sandy mess.

"If anybody has to dig anybody out," he told her, his own smile broad, "it'll be me. I think you took half the dune with you." He brushed off her back as she worked on her front, then moved a bit lower, and that was fun too, slapping the sand away.

"Going down again, aren't I," she said. "I could come off again. No real point in cleaning me up now, much as I can tell you're loving the excuse. I know what you're doing there, boy."

"And if you do come off," he said, giving her backside one last good slap, "I'll help clean you up again. I'm chivalrous like that."

They stopped again at Tapotupotu Bay for a swim, washed the sand off in the clear blue waters of the Tasman Sea, and she didn't mind that either, and neither did he, because he loved swimming with Reka, even though she was still faster than he was. A picnic lunch, wet hair, salt and sand and sea and sun, and the final five kilometers to the carpark.

Cape Reinga, as far as New Zealand went. The northernmost point of the North Island, the point where the Tasman to the west met the Pacific to the east in a churning line of mixing waters. The path along which the spirit flew when it left the body, when it left this world.

Te Rerenga Wairua, the Leaping-Off Place of the Spirits. To most, a tourist attraction. But to a Maori, the most sacred spot there was.

"Can't believe you've only been here once," he said when they'd left the crowd taking the easier paved route along to the lighthouse, were climbing the hill to the vantage point above.

"Mmm," she said abstractedly, looking down along the finger of land beyond, off-limits to every living soul, down to the single gnarled pohutukawa clinging to the cliff as it had done for eight hundred years. To the spot where both their souls would, one day, slip down into the sea and join their ancestors.

She stood there looking, and he knew what she was feeling, that the power of this place had infused her soul as it did his own. He wrapped his arms around her from behind, the way he had so long ago at Motuarohia, looked out with her, and their hearts beat in time with each other, in time with this place, with the heritage that stretched back in an unbroken line to the first wakas that had come ashore on this island six hundred years ago. To the people who had crossed that expanse of ocean in a journey so long, so arduous, so perilous that it made every other risk their descendants would take, any courage and honor they could ever show, pale in comparison.

They stood, silent, letting it fill them, then walked down the hill again to the stone-surrounded platform that housed the lighthouse, the last bit of ground that living feet could tread here.

Full of tourists, as always. He could hear French and German and Japanese and a few more languages, too. English as well, though there were few of the clipped accents that fell most easily on his ear.

"Thanks for bringing me," Reka said softly, leaning against the stone wall next to him, still looking out. "It's been a good day."

"I did it for a reason," he said, and if he'd ever been sure of anything, he was sure now.

"Oh?" She turned her head to look at him, a few tendrils of long dark hair escaping their messy knot and whipping in the ever-present wind, her generous mouth curved in a smile, her dark, liquid eyes full of humor. "Not just to watch me tumble off my sled?"

"Nah, not just for that, entertaining as it was." He smiled back, then was serious again, was pulling out the box he'd grabbed while her back was turned, there in the carpark. And right there, in front of the tourists and the ancestors and everybody, was sinking to a knee, feeling the stone under his bare skin, because this was the place, and this was the time. "To ask you to marry me."

He opened the box, revealed the ring he'd spent hours picking out a couple weeks ago in Johannesburg, and prayed that she'd like it, that she'd want it. He was glad he wasn't wearing a monitor just now, because he didn't want to admit how hard his heart was pounding, how short his breath was coming as he waited for her answer.

"So," he managed to say, "what do you think? I know we started out exactly wrong. Well, not we," he amended, "I. I did. But we've got the rest of our lives—I mean, I do. Bloody hell, I should have practiced this. I should have written it down." He took a deep breath and plowed on. "The rest of—my life, I mean, to finish right. I've got every day until I die to show you how much I care. And every day until I die to know you do, too. I need to know that, baby. I need you so much. So please. Marry me."

"Hemi," she said, and she was laughing, and crying a little too, he thought. The tourists were all watching now, he could tell, and he was still on a knee, and she hadn't answered, and his heart was galloping like a runaway horse.

She wasn't even bothering with the ring. She had his hand, was pulling him to his feet, was throwing herself into his arms and kissing him, holding him. Loving him.

And then, finally, she stepped back, took his face in her hands, and smiled. Just smiled, and his heart was so full, he wanted to shout with the joy of it.

"Give me a chance," she told him, her heart there to see in her eyes. The heart that was his, just like his was hers, and always would be. "Give me a chance to say yes."

The End

Sign up for my New Release mailing list at
www.rosalindjames.com/mail-list to be
notified of special pricing on new books,
sales, and more.

Turn the page for a Kiwi glossary and a
preview of the next book in the series.

a mini kiwi glossary

agro: aggravation

All Blacks, the ABs: New Zealand's international rugby team, and the country's biggest celebrities

back: One of the 7 rugby players who play—well, in the back, outside the scrum. They tend to be leaner and do more of the running and kicking, although all players do all jobs.

boatie: sailor

bollocks: balls (of the male variety)

brekkie: breakfast

bush: the (wild, uncultivated) countryside

Captain's Run: final training session, the day before a match

chat up: flirt

chips: French fries

chilly bin: ice chest

chuffed: pleased

conversion: kicking the ball between the posts after a try. Worth two points.

cuppa: a cup of tea; the universal remedy

dead: very. "Dead easy": very easy

do the business: do the job, get the job done

Domain: park; usually the main park in a town or city

dressing gown: bathrobe

earbashing: a talking-to, or just yammering on

first five: a first five-eighths, a rugby No. 10—the director of the offense, and the main goal-kicker

fizz, fizzie: soft drink

fizzing: excited, ready for action

footpath: sidewalk

footy: rugby, or a rugby ball

forward: One of the eight rugby players who form the scrum and do more of the pushing, shoving, and tackling, though all players do all jobs. Tend to be bigger and stronger than backs.

front, front up: square up, face up

Four Square: chain of small grocery stores in NZ

fullback: rugby position (back). Stands in—yes, the very back. Does a lot of long kicking and is the last line of defense.

get stuck in: commit; try your hardest

good as gold: perfect, good, fine

good fist, make a good fist of it: do a good job

greenstone: pounamu, jade—prized by Maori, used in pendants

haere mai: Welcome

hangi: Maori feast, cooked in an earthen pit in the ground.

harden up: toughen up. Standard NZ (male) response to (male) complaints: "Harden the f*** up!"

have a go: try

heaps: lots

holiday: vacation

hongi: forehead/nose-touching ceremonial greeting amongst Maori.

hooker: rugby position (forward). In the front row of the scrum. A tough, physical, battling position.

hoover: vacuum

into touch, kicked into touch: out of bounds (across the touchline—the sideline)

ITM Cup rugby, club rugby, provincial rugby: lower levels of rugby, below Super 15, which is the elite, and the All Blacks, who are the all-stars, the international squad

jandals: flip-flops, New Zealand's choice of footwear (along with gumboots)

joker: guy. Not humorous or derogatory, just "some joker"—some guy.

ka pai: good. "It's all ka pai": it's all good.

kai moana: seafood. New Zealand has no native mammals, and kai moana was an important staple of the early Maori diet.

kerfuffle: skirmish

kia kaha: Be strong, stay strong: an important Maori concept

kia ora: Hello; good day

kit: clothes. Get your kit off, get your gear off: get undressed.

Kiwi: A New Zealander. (The bird is a lower-case kiwi; the fruit is a kiwifruit.)

larking about: messing around

lock: rugby position (forward)

lounge: living room

Maori: The original inhabitants of New Zealand; a Polynesian people

marae: Maori communal/ceremonial meeting place

moko: extensive, complex Maori tattoo: normally on an arm & shoulder, possibly chest as well

Mozzie: A Maori Australian (or an Australian Maori)

nappy: diaper

no worries: it's all good; everything will work out. The Kiwi mantra.

Northland: the northern tip of New Zealand's North Island, north of Auckland. **The Far North:** the skinny part poking up at the very top.

out on the razzle: out on the town; drinking and partying

park, paddock: playing field (rugby). A paddock is a field (the sheep type).

pasteboard: cardboard

pavement: sidewalk

pissed: drunk. A piss-up: an event at which people do a lot of drinking.

plaster, sticking plaster: Band-Aid

pohutukawa: iconic New Zealand tree. Blooms with red bottle-brush blossoms at Christmas; the "New Zealand Christmas tree."

pushchair: stroller

rugby: Rough contact sport with no padding, and "New Zealand's national religion"

second-five, second five-eighth: rugby position (back). The player who does the most distributing of the ball—from the scrum and from the breakdown. A key strategic position.

Sevens: a speeded-up form of Rugby Union; played internationally

shag: have sex with

spew: vomit

sportsman: athlete

stonkered: drunk

Super 15, Super rugby: high-level rugby competition. Five teams from NZ, five from Australia, five from South Africa.

sweet as: great; nice. (Kiwis use "as" to mean "extremely")

tea: informal dinner

ticker: heart. "Heaps of ticker": lots of heart (courage).

togs: swimsuit (men or women)

touchline: sideline

try: a goal, in rugby; worth five points.

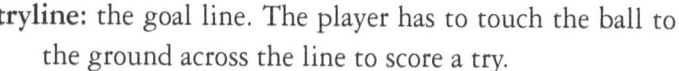

tryline: the goal line. The player has to touch the ball to the ground across the line to score a try.

try it on: flirt seriously, make a move on somebody

Under-19s: important international rugby competition for 18-year-olds

whanau: family; central Maori concept. Big whanau: extended family

wharekai: the dining room, more informal building at a marae

wharenui: the main ceremonial building at a marae

whinge: whine, complain. An unpopular thing to do in New Zealand. Harden up!

wing: rugby position (back). This is the one back position that is usually held by a big, tall guy. (There are two wings—left and right.) They tend to be the big power runners who can break tackles.

Find out what's new at the **ROSALIND JAMES WEBSITE.**
http://www.rosalindjames.com/

"Like" my **Facebook** page at facebook.com/ rosalindjamesbooks or follow me on **Twitter** at twitter.com/RosalindJames5 to learn about giveaways, events, and more. Want to tell me what you liked, or what I got wrong? I'd love to hear! You can email me at **Rosalind@rosalindjames.com**

by rosalind james

Cover design by Robin Ludwig Design In
http://www.gobookcoverdesign.com/

Read on for an excerpt from
Just This Once
Available now

prologue

♡

"Wow. Welcome to New Zealand."

Hannah said the words aloud. There was nobody around to hear her, after all. Despite the chill lingering in the morning air, she stood where she was for a few seconds more. The turquoise sea beckoned, its border of golden sand strewn with pale scallop shells left behind by the receding tide. It was exactly where she'd longed to be, these past weeks. And it was everything she'd hoped.

She dropped her towel and sandals and stepped into the cool water. Aiming towards the point at the far end of the bay, she delighted in her steady progress. Her mind settled down into the familiar rhythm, focused only on her strokes and her breath as the minutes went by.

Looking up at last to check her position, she felt a twinge of alarm. Had she not been swimming straight? The point was in the wrong place, wasn't it? She treaded water, turned in a circle. Realized with shock that she'd come much farther than she'd expected. What had felt like her own fast pace had in fact been a powerful current in the outgoing tide. One that was doing its best now to pull her out to sea.

No need to panic, she told herself firmly. All right, she was in some kind of rip tide. Now that she had stopped swimming, she could feel its strength. But she knew what to do, didn't she? She had to swim across it, that was all. This happened to people all the time. She would aim for a course parallel to the shore rather than trying to force her way directly back against the current's full power. Once she escaped the band of rip, she could turn back toward shore again. Back to safety.

She changed directions deliberately, swam strongly and steadily, working on maintaining her parallel course. Her progress, though, seemed discouragingly slow. The rip was wider than she had anticipated. It might even have shifted, a nervous little voice whispered in the back of her mind. She had heard that could happen.

She forced that treacherous voice back with an effort. She couldn't do anything about it now, other than what she was already doing. Keep swimming parallel, she told herself fiercely. She could swim for an hour without stopping, she knew. That meant she could swim even longer if she had to. Eventually, she would get out of this. Willing herself to stay calm, counting her strokes, she made it to one hundred, then two hundred.

And felt the change as she was caught by another, stronger rip. She had swum straight into it, and was once again being pulled out inexorably with the current.

The first stirrings of real panic shortened her breath. She forced the fear back, focused on breathing with her strokes, and began to count again. One hundred strokes, she told herself. Count. Breathe. But as she counted off sixty, then seventy, she could feel herself tiring, and knew she was losing the battle.

Where were the people? She hadn't seen a soul when she entered the water. Nobody knew where she was, and there was nobody to see her struggling. Nobody to help her. Nobody to save her.

How could this be happening?

All she had wanted was a vacation.

♡

www.ingramcontent.com/pod-product-compliance
Lightning Source LLC
Chambersburg PA
CBHW020308150626
46552CB00022B/2201